A 6-Year Affair

A 6-Year Affair

❖

The Post Graduate Educations of a
Scientist and of a Writer

A Novella

by

ROGER DERBY

Copyright © 2012 by Roger Derby.

Library of Congress Control Number:		2012918095
ISBN:	Hardcover	978-1-4797-2401-7
	Softcover	978-1-4797-2400-0
	Ebook	978-1-4797-2402-4

All rights reserved. No part of this book may be reproduced or transmitted in any form or by any means, electronic or mechanical, including photocopying, recording, or by any information storage and retrieval system, without permission in writing from the copyright owner.

This is a work of fiction. Names, characters, places and incidents either are the product of the author's imagination or are used fictitiously, and any resemblance to any actual persons, living or dead, events is entirely coincidental.

This book was printed in the United States of America.

To order additional copies of this book, contact:
Xlibris Corporation
1-888-795-4274
www.Xlibris.com
Orders@Xlibris.com

AUTHOR'S NOTES

Although real places and events are mentioned in the following story, all of the characters are purely imaginary.

The verses quoted by one of the central characters are from A. E. Housman's, *A Shropshire Lad*.

News of the death of his former mistress could not have come at a more inopportune time for William Schmidt. He had not been looking forward to his sixtieth birthday. Somehow sixty seemed so much older than fifty-nine. He had not planned to do much of anything about it other than take his wife Emily out to dinner. Because she had been working especially long hours of late, he suspected that she had forgotten all about it. As for his late-teenage daughters, who were away at college and very busy with studies and extra-curricular activities, he did not expect to hear much of anything from them except for a phone call or perhaps a card. His first suspicion that something was up occurred when they showed up early Saturday afternoon, Jennifer, down from New Haven and Isabel, up from New Brunswick. When he asked them about this previously unannounced weekend trip home they were evasive and mumbled something about helping their mother with some kind of project. His suspicions were further aroused when he discovered that his wife and the girls were busy working on something in the kitchen. When he asked them to tell him what was going, on his wife decided that it was time to tell him the truth.

"Will," she said, "We're having a surprise party for you. It'll be just us and the Wilsons and Bob Gentry and a girlfriend of his."

Jane Wilson was Will's editor at Taylor & Jones a small, but respected, publishing house in New York. Over a period of many years Jane had been an endless source of encouragement and good judgement. Her husband, Bob, was also involved in publishing; and the two couples had become good friends. Bob Gentry was a senior partner at the law firm where Emily had become a rising star and was something of a mentor to her. His friend, Teresa, was an unknown, but was reputed to be as sharp as she was attractive. In an instant Will's birthday blues disappeared. "Wonderful, thank you all," he said and hugged them all in turn.

"It'll be pretty simple, *coq au vin*, salad and dessert," Emily announced. "The girls are going to make the salad and dessert; I've already made the *coq au vin*. We're going to drink champagne straight through, French style."

A wave of good feelings and of contentment surged up within him. He liked everything he had heard about the evening to come. Just having his daughters home was a treat in itself. He was also happy to see their competence in the kitchen and eagerness to pitch in and help their mother.

He was also glad that Emily had not wanted to have the party catered. As hard as she was working on her blossoming career he would easily have understood, but would have found the presence of a caterer somewhat intrusive.

The guests arrived promptly at seven o'clock and began munching on *hors d'oeuvres* and sipping champagne. All of the women, including his daughters, had dressed up a bit for the occasion. Will thought they looked wonderful. He was particularly impressed with his wife's new dress.

A dark-blue velvet creation, it had more décolletage than any dress he had ever seen her wear in the twenty some years they had been together. Teresa, Bob Gentry's girl friend was wearing a bright orange sari and turned out to be as interesting as she looked.

A TV producer, she had just returned from Martinique where she and her colleagues had been filming a piece about the four-day carnival that precedes the beginning of lent. Not only did she have a healthy tan, but she was a skilled raconteur filled with interesting descriptions of costumes and customs.

The Wilsons were asking his daughters about college and they seemed to be basking in the attention. And they too looked marvelous. The oldest, Jennifer, was in a "basic black dress" which suited her young skin and blonde hair. Number two daughter had elected to wear a stunning dark-green suit. As he sat back sipping his champagne and admiring his guests, Will decided that he was just as glad not to know what the suit had cost. He also wondered what the jurors his, wife tried so hard to impress with her plain outfits, would think if they could see her in her velvet dress.

Unlike some lawyers who tried to put on an elegant and imposing appearance when they were in the courtroom, Emily did the exact opposite.

It was one of her many practices which Will found both charming and fascinating. On days when she was to appear in court she deliberately wore the cheapest, blandest, baggiest suits imaginable. Her shoes, made in England and incredibly expensive and deliciously comfortable, looked like something brought down from a grandmother's attic. An unbecoming hair style, a shabby purse purchased at a thrift shop and large horn rimmed glasses completed the picture. When Will asked her about this costume, her comments revealed that a lot of thought had gone into it.

"I don't want any woman on the jury being jealous of me," she told him. "I want them to identify with me. I want them to feel sorry for my client for having such a poor looking lawyer. And I don't want to look the least bit sexy. I want them to listen to my arguments, not study my body or my outfit or wonder about how much I am making per hour. And another advantage of looking mousy is that the opposition will underestimate you and get careless."

Emily's dressing down tactics seemed to be working very well. She had recently represented clients who had been injured by defective appliances and won substantial compensations for them from both vendors and manufacturers. Will, however, suspected that most of her success was due to her skill at cross-examination which he attributed in part to her innate quickness and in part to her meticulous preparation. The long hours she devoted to her career as a trial attorney prevented her from indulging in her one and only hobby, gourmet cooking.

She had become seriously interested in the subject during her junior year abroad spent living with a French family and studying at Grenoble. After their marriage, it became obvious to Will that as a busy young attorney and later as a new mother and part-time attorney, his wife should be free from most, if not all, responsibilities in the kitchen. He also realized that as a writer, he was in a much better position to control his schedule than she was hers. Hence, in the early years of their marriage, he did most of the cooking. Later as money began to come in from the sale of the movie rights to his first book, *Soldiers' Stories,* and from Emily's law practice, he decided to hire a part-time cook and even on occasions used a caterer. Later, when Emily decided that she wanted to go back to work full time, they hired a nanny. These arrangements had worked out well and being free of many domestic responsibilities they were able to pour their energies into their careers. On the few occasions when Emily did the cooking, she enjoyed it in a way that would have been impossible had circumstances required her to cook on a daily basis; Will's birthday was one such an occasion.

She chose to make *coq au vin* for several reasons. She knew that it was one of Will's favorites and that it could be prepared well-in-advance and simply warmed up in the oven just before serving. Under her tactful supervision, Jennifer prepared a large bowl of salad and a traditional vinaigrette dressing. Freshly baked French bread from a fancy local bakery would accompany the first course. Isabel made the birthday cake which was to be garnished with fresh strawberries.

While the guests were drinking their second glasses of champagne, Emily excused herself and went into the dining room to check on the table. Everything looked perfect, even to her critical eye. Next she went into the kitchen and found that the *coq au vin* had been sufficiently warmed in its large, colorful casserole. She removed it from the oven, carried it to the dining room and announced that dinner was ready.

"Bring your champagne glasses with you," she instructed.

Like everything else for the evening, the seating had been carefully planned. She placed the female guests next to Will and the male guests next to her. The girls sat facing each other in the middle of the table.

The *coq au vin* had just been served into bowls when the telephone rang.

Emily groaned. "What could that be?"

"Don't worry, Mother. I'll get it in the kitchen," Jennifer offered and left the room. A few moments later she returned and approached Will. "It's for you, Dad. It's Jack Billington. Says it's important that he speak to you for just a few moments."

As Will left the dining room for the kitchen to take the phone call he wondered what it could be about. He had known Jack Billington for over 40 years, ever since they had been in boarding school together. He had also known Jack's mother Prudence Billington far better then he had known her son, and though he occasionally thought about her, he had not seen her in many years.

In the kitchen he picked up the phone. "Hello, Jack. How are you?"

"Well, but I've got some sad news. Mother died last night, from leukemia. You were so close for so long that I thought you should know. There'll be an announcement in the *Times* tomorrow. I wanted you to hear about it first."

Will felt a tightening in his chest and stomach. Finally he was able to say, "Jack, that's so sad. It's hard to believe. She was never sick in all the years I knew her. And always so energetic."

"She was," Jack Billington replied. "There'll be a memorial service on Thursday."

"I'll be there. Thanks for calling me, Jack."

"I'm glad I caught you, Will. I've got to make some other calls. I'll see you at the service."

"Jack, pass along my condolences to everyone."

"Thank you, Will. Got to go now. Good bye."

Will put down the receiver and went to the kitchen sink and splashed cold water onto his face and took a deep breath. He did not feel like going back into the dining room to continue the party. It seemed wrong to be celebrating something when someone who had been so close to him had died. He thought of Emily and the efforts she had made. And the girls. Prudence's death was his problem, not theirs. He wasn't sure if any of them even knew who she was. "I owe it to them to keep a stiff upper lip and enjoy the party," he mumbled to himself. He took a drink of water from the faucet over the sink and returned to the dining room.

The following morning they slept late, until almost eleven o'clock. In the kitchen Emily prepared brunch while Will went out to get a copy of the Sunday *New York Times*. After gobbling down a substantial amount of scrambled eggs and Canadian bacon, they sat comfortably at their kitchen table drinking their second cups of coffee and reading the paper.

Will looked across the table at his wife and said, "That was a truly lovely party last night. I think everyone had a great time."

"I was a little worried about you for a moment," she replied. "When you came out of the kitchen after Jack Billington's call you looked a little funny. What was that all about?"

"Jack called to tell me about his mother's death. I've known the Billingtons for more than forty years."

"That seems a bit strange. Calling about his mother's death. I don't think you've seen Jack three times in the 20 years we've been married."

"That's true, but we were very close at one time."

"I see. Will you be going to the funeral?"

"There's going to be a memorial service on Thursday, but you don't have to go."

"I'd only go to keep you company. I've hardly ever seen Jack and never met his mother. Doesn't seem like there'd be much point in my going. And I've got a big court date on Friday."

"Sweet to offer, but there's no need for you to go."

"Are you sure?"

"Absolutely."

Emily nodded and continued to read a column in the business section of the *Times*. Will picked up the first section and quickly found Prudence Billington's obituary on the second to last page.

PRUDENCE BILLINGTON, 81, DISTINGUISHED MICROBIOLOGIST

By AGNES HUNTINGDON-SMITH

Prudence Billington, widow of Nobel Laureate Adam Sorenson, and distinguished microbiologist in her own right succumbed to leukemia at her home in Connecticut on April 14. She was 81. Mrs. Billington's first husband was the late Reginald Billington, the well-known investment banker. Because she had already published several important scientific papers under the name Prudence Billington, she elected not to change her name again following her marriage to the Swedish scientist Adam Sorenson.

Although Mrs. Billington did not begin her career as a microbiologist until her early fifties, she moved ahead rapidly in the scientific community, primarily, because of her work on the epidemiology of the bacterium *streptococcus pyrogenes* which she pursued while working as a postdoctoral fellow at the Center for Disease Control in Atlanta. The bacterium is associated with life- or limb-threatening infections often following puncture wounds. Mrs. Billington's interest in infectious bacteria originated during a visit to a U.S. Army hospital in Japan where she had gone to visit her friend the writer William Schmidt who had been evacuated to Japan after having received a serious wound during the Tet Offensive in the Vietnam War.

An honors graduate of Vassar with a degree in biology Mrs. Billington put her scientific career on hold following her marriage to Reginald Billington. She is survived by two sons of the marriage, John R. and Daniel G., both of this city. Another son, Peter, was killed in the early days of the Vietnam War.

Following her return to New York from Atlanta, she worked as a "bench scientist" for a number of years and continued to develop her expertise with staining techniques for micro-organisms. This work led to a collaboration with Adam Sorenson whom she later married. She was often a mentor to young women struggling to establish scientific careers and often co-authored scientific papers with them.

In addition to her sons Mrs. Billington is survived by three grandchildren.

After studying the obituary for some minutes Will put down the newspaper and sat staring out the kitchen window. Presently Emily looked up and noticed that he was not reading. "Will, what's up? By this time you're usually grumbling about some guy's stupid book review. You look a million miles away."

"I guess I am, far away in time. Here you better read this, you'll hear about it soon enough anyway," he replied and handed her the obituary.

Emily took the paper and studied it for a few minutes and said, "Will, I never knew you had a visitor in Japan. You never told me about it."

"My family was in no position to go and Prudence thought somebody should go. She was available and the cost was nothing to her. And following Peter's death she felt a special kind of duty to the wounded."

"How long did she stay?"

"Two months. She didn't just visit with me. One of the nurses suggested that she read to some of the other men. She did that and ended up staying for two months. She also became pals with the nurse who suggested it, Captain McMahan. Later they used to see each other back in the States."

"How come you never told me any of this?"

"That was from a different time, a different life. There are some things I just don't want to talk about."

"Not even with me? I didn't think we had any secrets from each other."

"There're some things which aren't exactly secrets, but you don't necessarily talk about them."

"Like what?"

"Well, lets say old boyfriends. You were 28 when we met. Surely you must have had some boyfriends. We never talked about them. You never brought them up and I certainly wasn't going to."

"I'd have told you anything you wanted to know."

"Frankly, I didn't think it any of my business. I felt, and still do, that if you thought there was any need for me to know something you would have told me."

"That's true. But this thing about you and the hospital comes as a surprise. I guess, like most lawyers and most wives for that matter, I don't like surprises. Now I know where you got all that information about biologists that's in your book about the drug company. Maybe I'll be a character in your next book."

"Not likely."

"Why not?"

"Characters in stories have to have flaws. You just don't have much wrong with you. You're weak in the flaw department."

"You don't think there's anything wrong with me?" Emily asked in a playful tone.

"Not much. You've got a mole that's really more like a beauty spot on your butt."

"Really, Will," she replied in mock exasperation. "Can't you do better than that?"

"Well, you have some of the faults that are typical of your profession. Sometimes you are too eager to win an argument with friends when you should just let something go."

"How come you never mentioned that before?"

"Because you are you and I love you just as you are."

"Really?"

"Yes, I wouldn't want you to change by one *iota*."

"You don't think I need some kind of self improvement program?"

"Absolutely not. The French have a proverb, *Le mieux, c'est l'ennemi du bien*."

"Better is the enemy of good. When I was at Grenoble the mother of the people who I was staying with used to say that, especially when she was trying to give me and her granddaughter lessons in pastry making. But where did you learn it? Certainly not in school."

Now Emily had really hit on a time in his life that he did not want to talk about. He also did not want to lie to her. He decided to finesse the question. "I always liked it. It reminds me of our, 'A camel is a horse designed by a committee'. Now go back to your paper while I read the book reviews."

"Okay," she replied and picked up the business section.

Will rustled around in the stack of papers until he found the book reviews, but instead of reading, he simply sat thinking of a winter day in the country many years earlier when he had stopped in at the Billington's summer home in Connecticut.

A year and a half after having his leg nearly blown off during the Tet offensive, ex-Lieutenant William Schmidt age 26 limped out of an army separation center and headed for New York. After two weeks of celebrating, drinking and gourmandizing, he dipped into the money that had been piling up during his months in the hospital and bought a fancy red convertible. He packed his few belongings and started a long and leisurely drive to Gainesville, Florida, where he would use his veteran's benefits to attend the university and work towards an advanced degree in English literature. He had picked a university in the deep south because he had been advised that cold weather would bother his leg, especially during the first year or two after the series of operations that had been required to repair it.

The first year of his program proceeded without any real problems. He enjoyed reading the required classics and writing critical comments about them. But after a year the atmosphere of the college began to seem more and more confining. Through a girlfriend he became interested in the problems of the migrant workers who harvest Florida's abundant crops of fruits and vegetables, and began to plan a book on the subject. He also thought more and more about his experiences and that of others who had spent months or even years in military hospitals recovering from wounds. In the end he decided to drop out of the doctoral program, settle for an MA degree and begin writing a book about the lives of severely wounded soldiers. He also decided to return to New York where he believed he would more easily be able to pick up suitable part time work. Upon learning of his plan one of his professors at Gainesville was able to arrange an introduction with a publishing house in New York. A job as a factchecker and proofreader resulted.

Will's original plan had been to write a non-fiction book and he spent long hours doing research. In the process he learned all kinds of surprising things about wounds. Surgeons, he discovered, are often more inclined to leave a piece of metal in a wounded soldier's head than to remove it in a dangerous operation. Contrary to intuition, wounds in which bits of clothing are driven into the body by a bullet or an explosion often tend to cause more problems than a simple metal fragment. He also learned all about the pain experienced by amputees from non-existent limbs and a lot about morphine and other pain relieving drugs. But in the end the book that began to emerge was not at all satisfying. Packed with details about all kinds of wounds and procedures for handling them, it began to seem more like a textbook than a testament about wounded soldiers and the men and women who take care of them. After months of reflection he decided that he could tell a more truthful and useful story in a work of fiction and began work on the novel which eventually became *Soldiers'Stories*, his first success.

It took almost two years working several evenings a week and half of almost every weekend to produce the first draft. His boss at the publishing company where he was still working as a factchecker suggested that he show it to a friend at Taylor & Jones and arranged an introduction. This was a lucky break which Will did not fully appreciate for many years; he was spared the frustration and agony experienced by aspiring writers who so often find it difficult to find anyone willing to read a manuscript much less publish it. The editor assigned to evaluate his novel was a young woman named Jane Wilson. Their first meeting took place at a Greek restaurant.

Jane Wilson arrived late and was so shabbily dressed in blue jeans and denim jacket that Will at first had trouble taking her seriously. He was also troubled by a complete lack of makeup and adornment of any kind. Dirty blonde hair and rimless glasses only made things worse. But she was evidently well acquainted with the restaurant and things got better fast.

"I'll be honest, Will, I'm a little bit nervous," she opened with candor. "You're my first writer. I've just been promoted from proof reading. I'll bet you're a little bit nervous too."

"I am," Will admitted.

"Okay, let's start with something to relieve the tension. We should have a glass of *retsina*."

"I'm game, but what is it?"

"Greek red wine. Tastes like turpentine. Goes well with lamb."

While they were waiting for the wine she jumped right into the subject of the meeting. "Will, I've got to tell you that I loved your book and that old Mr. Taylor has read it and he likes it almost as much as I do."

Because Will had been primed to expect some rejection he was almost too surprised to say much of anything more interesting than, "Holy smoke."

"The news isn't all good."

"Oh, what does that mean?".

"It's not that bad. But you need to make some revisions, cut out some of the more gruesome details. There's too much about bedpans and the problems of wiping your ass when you're missing a hand. We're not saying that everything should be sugarcoated. On the contrary. We like the honesty and the obvious authority of the book. But we want to sell it. We don't want people to be so sad or grossed out that they won't recommend it to their friends."

"I can accept that. But I don't want my book to be overly sanitized or filled with euphemisms."

"We don't either," she replied.

The waiter arrived at this point and again Jane took charge. "You've got to have the *soulvaki*."

"What's that?"

"Lamb chunks on a skewer. You'll love it."

He agreed and she ordered two *soulvakis* and another round of *retsina*.

The wine affected Jane every bit as much as it did Will. At one point she told him that her favorite part of the book had been a love scene between an amputee and a nurse. "Obviously I'm not a man," she said and smiled, "but somehow I can understand the soldier's worry about not being able to have an erection and the relief he felt when the nurse restored his confidence in his manhood. That was very moving."

Near the end of the luncheon conversation turned back to practical matters. Jane produced a large manila envelope and explained that it contained a list of suggestions for a revised manuscript and a draft of a contract. "I believe that Mr. Taylor will go for a $5,000 advance. Look it all over and plan to come in, meet him, and sign the contract. How about next week?"

When the advance money was finally in his hands Will decided to work full time on the revisions and gave notice to his boss at his fact-checking job.

He also decided to spend a month or so in an isolated place where interruptions and distractions would be at an absolute minimum. Suddenly the idea of going to a summer resort in winter occurred to him. What could be more deserted? But the only summer resort Will knew anything about was Rocky Cove in Connecticut where he had visited the Billington family during summer vacations from prep school. Will remembered that some of the houses at the resort had been winterized so that they could be used as holiday retreats. Perhaps a short-term rental could be arranged. Only a few long distance phone calls to a realtor in New London were required. The only problem remaining was transportation. Not wanting to be a car owner in New York he had sold his beloved convertible before leaving Florida.

He decided that the best thing would be to go to New London by train and buy an old jalopy that he could sell or scrap when his two-month sojourn at Rocky Cove was over.

On a deceptively warm, late-January afternoon Will drove his new old pickup truck into the driveway of a rambling summerhouse with a magnificent view of Long Island Sound. The house had belonged to a retired college professor who had recently died and the heirs were delighted to have someone living in the house while arrangements were being made to sell it. Will unloaded his electric typewriter, his suitcase and about a week's worth of groceries and was soon ready to start on the revisions.

Things went smoothly for the first two weeks. When he studied the list of suggestions given to him by Jane Wilson he realized that most of them were quite reasonable and easy to follow. Slowly, but carefully, he went through the complete manuscript page by page making additions or deletions with a red pencil. When he had finished he simply sat down and started typing a new draft. He was very disciplined in his approach; he divided the day into three two-hour work sessions and kept religiously to this schedule. He also made a point of making regular, simple meals and exercising by walking on the beach every afternoon. Time not spent on typing, exercising or cooking was given over to reading *You Can't Go Home Again*, a nice, long, fat book he had always wanted to read. On the tenth day of this regimen the weather began to change.

First, the temperature began to drop and things stayed very cold for several days. Next, a moisture-laden storm proceeded eastward from the Great Lakes and began to dump snow in record quantities all over New England. The storm, which came to be known as The Valentine's Day Storm, paralyzed communities everywhere and resulted in numerous power failures. Particularly hard hit were thinly populated rural areas and summer colonies not prepared to handle the unusual amount of snow. Rocky Cove was no exception.

Before the snow stopped falling more than a foot had accumulated on the roads around and into the old resort. Will had no problem with the snow. He had, he figured, more than enough food for a week; the new furnace in the old house worked well and he was as comfortable as he would have been in New York. Then the electric power failed.

Without electric power his fancy electric typewriter, with its marvelous self-correcting features, was useless. Without power the electric blowers which circulated hot air from the furnace stopped and the furnace turned itself off. And there was no electric light to read by. But there was a fireplace and a reasonable supply of wood stacked in the garage.

For two days Will sat by the fire. During the days when there was enough light he continued reading *You Can't Go Home Again*. At night he used an oil lamp which he had discovered in the garage along with certain emergency supplies the old professor had gathered in anticipation of a severe storm or a hurricane. Fearing that pipes might freeze he kept a steady trickle of water running in one of the bathrooms. On the third day he began to get cabin fever.

Outside it was clear and cold, but the sun was shining brightly. In a closet just inside the front door he found an old fashioned pair of goulashes and decided that the owners wouldn't mind if be borrowed them, and an old walking cane as well. The only hat he had on hand was an old baseball cap.

He put it on, wrapped a dishtowel around his neck to serve as a scarf, donned his shabby old overcoat, and set out to explore snow-covered Rocky Cove.

The going was not quite as difficult as he had expected. The wind in the night had blown much of the snow off the roads into drifts along fences and hedges. He shuffled along enjoying the fresh air and the eerie absence of sound. Here and there the low lying winter sun cast intriguing shadows of bare trees onto the immaculate snow. As he passed the summer homes impeccable in their white coverings he saw no sign of life. On some of them long, glistening icicles hung from eves and gutters.

In the road there were no tire tracks, not even a sign of a maintenance vehicle or a snow plow. He suddenly wished that he had a companion to share this scene. He had trudged on about another quarter of a mile when his leg began to trouble him and had decided to turn back when he noticed what looked like steam or smoke rising up from a house some one hundred yards ahead. He pushed on to find out what it really was. As he drew closer he began to sense something familiar about the place. Suddenly he realized it was the Billington place he had visited during several summer vacations more than a decade ago. In the driveway there was a station wagon almost invisible in a snowdrift. A closer look at the house revealed that something was indeed coming out of a chimney. Surely somebody must be there. Perhaps it was his old friend Jack. He shuffled through the snow surrounding the house and knocked vigorously on the door.

After what seemed like a very long time a window was opened and a woman leaned out and shouted, "Who's there? What do you want?" It was Prudence Billington.

Will shouted back, "It's me! Will Schmidt."

The window closed with a bang and in a few moments the door was flung open and Prudence Billinton's strong arms were around him.

"Will, I can't believe it. What are you doing here?"

"I'm renting Professor Harrington's house while I do the revisions on my book. I was out walking and saw what I thought was smoke coming out of a chimney. Decided to investigate. What are you doing here?"

"Not much. Came up to check on the house and to do some serious thinking. Got caught by the storm."

"What was the smoke I saw? Does your furnace work?"

"No, it went out when the power failed, but I've got a gas stove that works and gas logs in the library. Come on into the kitchen and get warm. I keep the oven on most of the time."

The heat from the oven and the sunlight streaming in through the south facing windows made the room warm and inviting. When Will removed his coat and Prudence saw his dish towel scarf she burst out laughing and hugged him again. "I can't offer you much lunch. I'm almost out of food, but I can give you a cup of tea."

As he sat savoring the hot drink he looked across the table and marveled at the beautiful woman sitting there. Shiny-black, jaw-length hair framed a face with an oriental cast. Smooth, healthy skin. Neatly cut bangs and brown eyes. Full, well-proportioned lips and good, well-cared-for teeth. He did some rapid mental arithmetic. When he had been sixteen she had had three teenaged children. She must have been at least thirty seven or thirty eight. Thirteen years ago. She must be approaching fifty. Hard to believe.

On the other side of the table Prudence was admiring her unexpected guest. The big, handsome boy who had been a friend of her children had turned into an irresistible man, even more appealing now than when she had visited him in the hospital, almost five years ago. A hint of gray at the temples and residual evidence of difficult days showed in the lines in his face and made him seem older and more mature than his twenty-nine years.

Between the cold walk and living for several days in a chilly environment Will had become ravenous and thought of food. "You say you're low on food. I've got a fair amount. Why don't I go bring it here? You provide the heat and I'll provide the food."

"Will, you won't have to persuade me. But how will you bring it? I don't think a car could get through."

"I'll carry it. I've got an old suitcase. I'll bring the food in it."

"Is that practical? How far is it?"

"Less than a mile."

"I'll come with you."

"You don't have to."

"I want to. I've got plenty of warm clothes and boots."

"I'd welcome the company."

Within minutes they were bundled up and out the door. When they were about halfway back to the professor's house they paused to admire the mysterious shapes made by snow-covered hedges and bushes, and to wonder at the silence. As they turned to continue their expedition Will reached out and took Prudence's hand and they marched on hand-in-hand without speaking. After they had gone a short distance Will stopped and pulled her gently toward him. "I hope I'm not being dumb or stupid. I long to hug you."

"I'm very glad you do." she answered. "I've wanted to do more than hug you."

After a long embrace Will spoke into a flap-covered ear. "That was wonderful. I don't want to spoil anything, but I want to kiss you."

Her only answer was to put her gloved hands behind his head and pull it down so that she could kiss him squarely on the lips.

When they parted Will was so thrilled that he could hardly speak. "I feel like I'm ten feet tall and sixteen years old. I don't know what to say."

"I feel like a teenager too," she answered. "And like a teenager I'm getting awfully hungry."

Again, hand-in-hand, they ploughed on to the old professor's house. Once there they hastily loaded Will's suitcase and two pillowcases with groceries and headed back. The return trip was heavy going. They carried the suitcase between them, sharing the load, and each of them carried a pillow case thrown over a shoulder.

By the time they had reached the Billington house Will's leg was beginning to give him real trouble. Almost two miles in the cold and snow was too much and the heavy load of groceries had only made matters worse. But he was determined not to show any sign of weakness in front of Prudence and tried not to limp. He noted that her stamina appeared to be undiminished and wasn't sure how to feel about it. Should he feel belittled because a woman had more stamina, an older woman for that matter? Or should he feel admiration at her evident strength and fitness? Almost as soon as they were in the door she settled these questions.

"Sit down Will," she said. "I don't have pieces of metal and screws in my legs. I'll make some soup." It came quickly and was followed by a ham omelet that consumed exactly one third of their eggs. Dessert was an orange which was a special treat for Prudence who had had no fruit, fresh or canned, since the first day of the storm. The final touch was a cup of instant coffee sweetened with condensed milk. Prudence said that she had never welcomed a cup of coffee so much in her life. After she had finished she scooped up the dishes, went to the sink, and turned on the water.

Will watched for a few moments and then jumped up and shouted, "You've got hot water? How come? Mine went out with the power."

"We've got a gas water heater. All I had to do was light the pilot light."

Will moved beside her at the sink and put his hand into the hot running water. She looked at him and said, "Will you could shave if you want to, you could even have a bath."

"On my God. A bath," he blurted out. "Prudence, you're wonderful." He pulled her towards him and hugged her. As she returned his hug his hands drifted downward onto her buttocks.

She pushed gently on his chest and said, "Hey, old soldier, what're you doing?"

"Sorry," he said and removed his hands.

"I didn't say to stop," she answered and laughed. "Go have your bath!"

The tub was as he had remembered it from his previous visits, an enormous, claw-footed, cast iron relic from a bygone era. As he turned a large, old-fashioned handle hot water gushed out of the brass faucet from which ancient nickel plating had worn away. A rubber drain plug was attached to the end of the tub by a chain. In a few spots the white enamel had been chipped away revealing a dark-blue undercoating. A real sponge, bigger than a big man's hand sat in a wire soapdish fixed to the side of the tub. When the water was almost a foot deep Will eased himself into it. He submerged his aching leg and then, as the water continued to deepen, his whole body, up to his chin.

After some minutes of soaking he sat up and grabbed the giant sponge and began to rub it gently on his limbs and face, a fascinating mixture of compliance when squeezed, and slight roughness when dragged across the skin. Will was marveling at this strange natural material when there was a knock at the door.

It opened a crack and Prudence called in, "Are you modest? Can I come in?"

"Not any more," Will shouted back. "Come on in."

She entered and sat near the tub on an old wooden stool. "Last time I saw you your leg was in an ankle-to-hip cast. But, from what they told me, I had the idea that it would turn out all right in the end."

"It's not perfect, but it works pretty well. Want to see it?"

"I do. I hope that doesn't sound insensitive. When you're fond of somebody I guess it's legitimate to be concerned and curious"

"Back in Japan you earned the right to be curious"

He raised his leg from the water and drooped it over the edge of the tub. "I had four operations, but there're only three scars because they went into one place twice. It got quite withered from all the time in casts and braces. It's still not quite as big as the other one. They told me the best thing I can do is to use it regularly and sensibly. I do."

Prudence ran her hand over the scars and then examined them. She squeezed his calf muscles. "You know how Peter died?" she asked as she eased his leg back into the water.

"Yes, a land mine."

"It blew his lower leg completely off. They got a tourniquet on it, but he died of shock at the aid station."

Will found himself at a loss for words. He wanted to say something comforting, but was afraid that something foolish or trite would be worse than nothing. After a few moments of silence he said, "It seems especially sad when someone so promising dies so young."

Prudence wiped away a couple of tears. "Peter's death was much more painful than Reggie's. It was sad, but the death of a sixty-two-year old man is just not the same as the death of a twenty-two-year old with a full life in front of him."

Will nodded and said, "I saw a lot of it and some things worse than death."

Prudence rose from the stool and stood over Will. She reached down and ran her hand through his hair. "I'm sorry you had to suffer so much and I'm so relieved you made it back. You've got a long bright future."

"Thank's. When my book's published I plan to put the war behind me. But for now, I want to speak for the thousands who spent months and even years in army hospitals."

"A good goal. I'm not going to forget Peter and Reggie, but I need to get on with my life. Let's not talk about death anymore."

"I agree," he said in a firm voice as he reached up with both hands and took her hand from where it was still resting gently on his head. "Prudence," he said, "Do something imprudent. Get in the tub with me."

She looked down at the strong and handsome man in the enormous tub of hot water and suddenly found the idea irresistible. "That doesn't sound imprudent. It sounds like a good idea. But first, I'm going to put in some lavender."

She went to a storage cabinet in the corner of the bathroom and came back with a jar of crystals that she sprinkled liberally into the bath. "Good for aching joints. Smells good too."

She put the lavender back into the cabinet and began to undress. "Suddenly I feel very shy," she called from across the room.

"You've nothing to be shy about. Come on, the water's fine."

Once shed of her last stitch of clothing all feelings of shyness disappeared and were replaced by a sense of freedom. She found that she welcomed the chance to show off her body and marched proudly across the bathroom and climbed into the tub.

In all his twenty-nine years Will had never seen anything he thought so beautiful as her naked body. He reached out to where she sat with her back towards him and gently pulled her against his chest. He kissed the top of her head. "Nothing like this has ever happened to me before," he told her in a voice taut with emotion.

"That makes two of us. I've never done anything even remotely like this."

Will pulled her closer and rested his chin on the top of her head. They sat quietly in this position for some time. Finally Prudence broke the silence. "The water's getting cold," she said and slithered forward in the tub to turn on the tap. In a few moments the water was hot again. "I like the way we were," she said and slid backwards until her head was once again under Will's chin. "This is a perfect start to my new life."

"This is perfect," Will agreed.

"Can I tell you what I've been thinking about?"

"Do I have a choice? Here I am held captive in the corner of an old tub, what can I do but listen?"

"I'm serious Will. I want you to listen and tell me if what I've been thinking sounds silly."

"Of course I'll listen and do anything else you want."

"Good. First, I'm tired of being so dutiful, so prudent. I'm tired of always putting everybody else's needs first, ahead of mine. I was a dutiful wife. I think I was a conscientious mother. I do a fair amount of good works in the city. But there's a part of me that has been put on the back burner. I feel like now is the time to bring it forward, let it out. Men have mid-life crises, why shouldn't I?"

"No reason. Is there anything you specially want to do?"

"This'll sound silly."

"Before you even say it, I know it won't be silly."

"Thanks. You knew that I'd majored in biology?"

"Actually, I didn't."

"Well I want to go back to school and study microbiology. Ever since I was in tenth grade I've loved looking at things under the microscope. I want to do that again. Does that sound silly?"

"Not at all. Only thing silly is thinking that it'd sound silly."

"That's sweet, Will, but I'm almost fifty years old."

"So what? When I was in Gainesville there were graduate students older than you are. And they did fine."

"Is that really true?"

"It is. Your only problem is going to be picking the right school. That'll depend on what your long-range goals are. Do you want to go for your Ph.D.? If you're in biology, that's a good idea. Not so important if you were, say, in engineering. Or in my case, I saw no great need to get a Ph.D. in literature. But for biology, I think it's a *sine qua non* if you want to call the shots. Otherwise, you'll end up following through on somebody else's plan."

"I definitely want to call the shots. But the exams. Could I pass them?"

"Without a shadow of a doubt. If you get into a program and you're bright, motivated, have some self-discipline you'll get through. Almost invariably the people who don't finish aren't really interested in their research topic."

"But could I get in?"

"Absolutely. I'd bet you did well in college."

"I did graduate with honors."

"I'm not the least bit surprised. As for the schools, the profs need graduate students. I will say this: there have undoubtedly been some changes in the curriculum since you went to college. You may have to make up a few courses, but you'd probably find them interesting."

"Will, you've almost convinced me."

"By the time the snow melts and we can get out of here I'll have you completely convinced. Your future is microbiology. It's inevitable."

She rose and stepped out of the tub and started to dry herself with a luxuriously thick towel. Will watched, enthralled.

"There's something else that's inevitable," she said, "and it's going to happen very soon. But you need to shave first. I don't want you scratching me. There's a razor in the medicine cabinet and there's a terry cloth robe on the hook behind the door. I'm heading for the library. That's where the gas logs are."

Within a very short time Will was beside Prudence in a foldout bed.

"I am kind of nervous," she said. "I'm not very experienced. I've never had an affair before."

"I'm sure no Don Juan," he replied. "I'm probably more nervous than you are."

They need not have worried.

The following morning they were ravenous and opened a small canned ham and ate thick slices along with two of their remaining eight eggs. They split an orange and, again, thoroughly enjoyed instant coffee with condensed milk. After breakfast they folded up the sofa bed and sat next to each other in front of the gas logs and talked and talked.

Prudence told Will about the death of her husband who had died from a stroke while they were cruising on a chartered yacht. After fruitless attempts to revive him she had single handedly brought the yacht back to port.

She asked Will if he minded talking about Vietnam and when he said that he didn't mind talking with her, she asked him many questions. She also expressed a keen interest in reading a draft of *Soldiers'Stories*.

"I'd welcome your opinion," he told her. "If I'm going to be your guest until the power comes on I'm going to need some clean clothes. Why don't I go get some clothes and bring back the manuscript at the same time?"

"Sounds good, but you aren't exactly a guest."

"What am I then?"

"You're my lover. I've never had a lover before."

"Me a *lover*! Does that make you my mistress?"

"I guess it does. That has a nice, naughty ring to it, like being some old king's girlfriend."

Will returned with the manuscript and clean clothes in the early afternoon and promptly requested permission to have another bath. While he sat savoring the hot water in the great tub, Prudence sat by the stove in the kitchen reading his manuscript. When he emerged from the bathroom, almost an hour later, he found Prudence still reading, but with tears in her eyes. "Where are you?" he asked.

"The nurse and the amputee making love."

"If it made you weep, I guess my writing's not so bad."

"Your writing's fine."

"But do I have it right? You were there, in Japan. Is the atmosphere right? Are the characters convincing?"

"You've got everything right. I love the nurse. She's almost like Captain McMahan."

"She's part composite and part pure invention."

"I think Captain McMahan will like it."

"I hope she'll see it in some book store and write to me."

"She'll see it. I'll send it to her when it comes out. She's retired. Lives in Knoxville, down in Tennessee."

"How do you know that?"

"I kept up with her. She married a surgeon and lives in a big house on a river that looks like a lake. I even visited her."

And so the afternoon passed as they moved from talk of mutual acquaintances to losses and disappointments and on to hopes and dreams for the future. After a light dinner carefully prepared from their remaining food they once again made love in the fold out bed by the gas logs in the library. They awoke during the night to find that the electric power had been restored and that lights were on all over the house. In the morning when Will mentioned that he could now use his electric typewriter Prudence suggested that he cut his work day to one, three-hour session and continue to eat and sleep at her house. Will readily agreed and set off enthusiastically for the old professor's house, a thermos of coffee under his arm. He found everything in order and was pleased that with the restoration of power the furnace had come on and the house was at a comfortable temperature. The typing went well and Will was in a happy mood as he headed back to Prudence. He found her in front of the house pushing snow off of her old station wagon. All smiles, she hugged him and kissed him on the cheek.

How wonderful it must be to have a wife to come home to he thought as they walked hand-in-hand toward the house.

"The radio says there's warmer weather coming. We'll be able to get out of here," she informed him.

He stopped and pulled her close. "I haven't minded being stranded here with you. These have been some of the happiest days of my life. I don't want this to end."

"It doesn't have to end. You can be my lover in New York."

"And you can do graduate school in New York. And I'll start on my next book."

By late spring Prudence had already been accepted by two universities to work for an advanced degree in biology. With the revisions of *Soldiers' Stories* behind him, Will submerged himself in another project.

As Will had predicted, Dr. Richard Cohen, the director of the program into which Prudence had been admitted, insisted that she take some courses during the summer to help her understand recent developments in the field. Unlike many women pursuing advanced degrees in science or engineering Prudence did not run into any sexual discrimination until it was too late to matter. This piece of luck was largely due to Dr. Cohen: with three bright daughters and a psychiatrist for a wife there was no way he could be anything but supportive. If there were any male members of his department who harbored anti-woman feelings, they were wise enough to keep them to themselves.

One of the courses picked out by Dr. Cohen was an accelerated organic chemistry course for premedical students. The other was an introduction to biochemistry. When she arrived back at her apartment with the heavy textbooks under her arm and had looked them over she found them so intimidating that she was on the verge of dropping out of the program on the very first day. As she was pondering her situation, Will telephoned and announced that he had good news, he was about to receive a substantial check from Taylor & Jones. From the tone of her voice he immediately sensed her worry and told her that he was on his way.

"Don't panic," he advised her. "Trust me. The other students are probably as scared as you are. The first few days will be the hardest. Like anything, you've got to start by learning the vocabulary. No brains required. Just some time. Do at least some studying every day. Make friends with some of your classmates and form a study group. Quiz each other. Explain things to each other. And, to be blunt, you've got a lot going for you."

"Such as?" she replied, her tone bordering on the pugnacious.

"First, unlike a lot of students you have absolutely no financial worries. Second, you have no family to worry about. Your children are grown and are doing well. Third, living in the city you have no transportation problems, no car to keep up or worry about on a cold morning. Fourth, you've got a lot of energy. You're as strong and healthy as a horse. Fifth, you're bright. I don't know how bright, but I'd bet my fat check you're bright enough. And last . . . I don't know how to put this. I saw it myself when I was a graduate student. Often spouses get in the way. They may be demanding or they may be sick and require help. You don't have any such responsibility. You are free to become a microbiologist or almost anything else within reason."

"After that kind of pep talk how can I go wrong?"

"You might go wrong, but I don't think you will. Why don't you start in by reading the introductions to your books? Then look over the first chapters. Check out the appendices, if there are any. Look for a glossary. While you're doing that I'll go bring in dinner."

Within a few weeks they settled into a routine which was to last somewhat longer than three years. Rather than move in together they each kept their separate apartments and devoted most nights to writing and study. Friday and Saturday nights were the exceptions which they invariably spent together, sometimes at Prudence's well appointed apartment, sometimes at Will's much more humble place. When Prudence's friends invited her to come to dinner she almost always turned down the invitation unless it was for a Friday or a Saturday. She always requested that Will be included and he always was.

She sharpened her friends' interest in Will by telling them, "I must tell you, I am Will's mistress and that I'm really enjoying it; it's a new experience for me." In referring to their situation she never used the word *relationship* which was then coming into vogue. She hated the word. "It sounds too damn mechanical and it sure as hell isn't euphonious," she indignantly told one of her old school friends.

Prudence's first success as a graduate student came when she easily passed the language requirement. The institute's policy was to require all candidates for a doctorate to pass an examination in a foreign language appropriate to their field of study. The test was usually of the "open-the-book-anywhere" type. According to this procedure a candidate would, with the approval of the examiner, select a book in the appropriate foreign language and be prepared to translate a selection taken at random from the book. On the day of the examination the candidate would bring the book to the examiners office where it would be opened to some page, usually near the middle, and the candidate would be told to translate.

When Prudence mentioned the requirement to Will he was full of good advice. "It's all in choosing the right book," he told her. "Pick a book on a subject you already know something about and one with plenty of illustrations." Having had three years of French in boarding school and two years at Vassar Prudence made the obvious decision to present a book in French. She chose *Traité de Zoologie, Protozoaires*. The examiner was so impressed with her performance that he wrote a special memorandum about it to Dr. Cohen.

Because New York did not seem to be the place to write a book about migrant farm workers Will put that project on the backburner and made a study of the garment district which he found an endless source of fascination. At first he concentrated on working conditions and safety. He learned all about the origins of the unions. Later, through a friend of a friend, he was introduced to some of the district's entrepreneurs and learned about the financial risks and some of its strange customs such as the 'factoring' or selling of accounts receivable to help finance the next season's production. Out of this research would come his second novel, *Scissors & Pins*, a love story based in the garment district.

Everything was not always smooth sailing. Occasionally, especially during their first year, Prudence would be upset by a mediocre score on an examination and would require reassurance and encouragement. Dr. Cohen would often become Will's ally on such occasions. They had met at a party given by a group of graduate students and had started off their conversation on a strange note. "I was prepared to dislike you," the professor told him. "When I first heard about you I thought you would turn out to be some kind of parasite or, at best, a drag on Prudence's progress. Then I found out from her that you were the one who encouraged her to go to graduate school and that without you she wouldn't be here. Let me tell you, she's talented, especially in the lab and as far as I'm concerned that's what really counts. She's fast, but not careless. Knows exactly what she's doing. And she often is quietly helpful to other students."

"Not surprised to hear any of this," Will told him. "I am grateful to you for confirming my own judgement, especially since I'm no scientist."

"I wouldn't ask you this except that we've both had a few drinks," the professor continued, "but are you in love with her?"

"That's a pretty personal question, but I'll answer it very directly. Yes, I'm in love with her. Very much."

"Good. Then you won't get in her way. You'll help her be what she can be?"

"I will."

"Everybody stubs their toe once in a while. Prudence is no exception. When she does, you hang in there and give her all the encouragement you can."

"I already have and I'll continue to do so."

"Good. Now let me tell you what's coming up. She has to pass her qualifiers. You know, the comprehensive exams. That's her biggest worry. When she gets through those she'll start on her dissertation. Because she's good in the lab she'll sail through the dissertation, unlike a lot of the ABD's I see."

"ABD?"

"Sorry, that's academic shorthand for 'all-but-dissertation'."

"Back to the qualifiers. Is there anything special she should do?"

"The test is given by a committee. Here's what I did years ago. I made a list of the favorite topics of each member of the committee and a list of embarrassing questions they might ask. Then I prepared answers to each of these hypothetical questions. It worked pretty well. It was good for my confidence and helped me organize my time. And, as it turned out, actually helped me answer a few questions."

"I'll pass the idea along to Prudence."

"You do that. Got to talk to some other folks. Glad to have met you," he said and offered Will his hand.

Within a few days of the party Prudence began to make her list. There would be five professors involved in administering her qualifier, a two-hour oral examination. After some study and reflection she decided to assign ten "embarrassing" questions to each professor. Next, she prepared an answer for each question and recorded her answers on file cards. In preparing her list she emphasized subjects about which she felt somewhat awkward. Where important equations were involved she made a point of knowing exactly where they came from. She made sketches illustrating the optics of traditional light microscopes and circuit diagrams for electron microscopes. She prepared herself to give clear explanations of the applications of the theories of probability to epidemiology. As the months went by she added many more questions to the original list and she came to enjoy the project. Her confidence soared.

When the big day finally came after two academic years and two summer sessions it was no anti-climax. Both her confidence and knowledge would be challenged. Several of the professors on the committee did not know her very well and suspected that a beautiful fifty-plus-year-old woman might be some kind of dilettante. Hence their initial questions were probes to find weak points. When they found that she was surprisingly well prepared one of them said, "I'd like to take this a few steps farther and find out exactly what your limits are, Miz Billington." There were no protests from other members of the committee; their curiosities had also been piqued. Thus Prudence found herself fielding questions far more difficult than any she had expected. The worst involved actually doing some calculations involving conditional probabilities on the blackboard. Others involved the design of experiments and pitfalls to be avoided. When she had impressed the committee with her knowledge of these subjects the questions turned to matters of hardware. Again, she impressed the interlocutors. Finally, Dr. Cohen, acting as chairman, interrupted and pointed out that other committee members had questions.

When the one female on the committee, who had at first been somewhat antagonistic to Prudence, began to sense an undercurrent of misogyny in the relentless probing by her male colleague she became impatient and decided to change tactics. Instead of asking questions designed to stump the candidate she began to ask questions whose answers she was sure Prudence could handle and which would impress the committee. Although she had no trouble answering these questions the whole process continued to be grueling. Again Dr. Cohen intervened and announced that he had a few questions of his own. Fortunately for the flagging Prudence his questions, somewhat like those of his immediate predecessor, were designed to show off the scholarship of his prize student. He limited his questions to subjects that he knew to be of special interest to Prudence. Mostly they pertained to the history of microbiology with questions covering such arcane topics as the performance of the microscopes used by early investigators. He even asked her about Anton van Leeuwenhoek. Prudence did not disappoint him. Exactly two hours after the examination had begun he called a halt to the proceedings and asked Prudence to wait in an adjoining room while the committee deliberated. She did not have long to wait. Within a few minutes she was called back and informed that the committee was in unanimous agreement: she had done well. Each member offered a hand in congratulations. Dr. Cohen suggested that she sit down for a few more minutes and tell the committee about her plans for a dissertation.

"I'm hoping to work in micropaleontology. I've long been interested in *foraminifera,* ever since I first read about them back as an undergraduate and then actually saw them under a microscope," she began.

"Why the special interest in fossils?" one of the committee members interrupted her. "Sounds dull."

"On the contrary," she responded enthusiastically. "Not only are they beautiful, but their enormous variety reflects something about early life and perhaps about life in general. I just can't help being curious about them."

"Even if that's not my cup of tea," he came back, "I think your interest and curiosity will take you a long way."

"What about the logistics of your project, have you thought about that? Where will you get the specimens?" another inquired.

"I have," Prudence responded. "The Museum of Natural History, right here in New York, has an excellent collection available for researchers."

"I think the committee would be interested to hear about the possible approach you told me about," chimed in Dr. Cohen.

"My idea is to use some of the new shadowing techniques used with the electron microscope to bring out fine structure that's never been seen before"

"What would that prove?"

"I think it would give valuable clues to the chemical and biological nature of ancient seas," Prudence answered confidently.

"Have you done any literature search yet?"

"Actually I have. There's a fairly recent source in German called *Grundzüge des zoologgischen Mikropaläontologie der Protozoen* by a guy called Pokorný. It's very comprehensive."

"*Sprechen Sie Deutsch?*" one member inquired.

"*Ein wenig,*" Prudence modestly replied. "My late husband and I spent two years in Germany right after the war. He encouraged me to learn German, but I never thought I'd be using it for something like this."

"That's a part of Miz Billington's preparation I wasn't aware of," Dr.Cohen announced. "She did the language requirement in French. The German only confirms my belief that she is well prepared to undertake her research. I now hereby close this meeting."

When Prudence arrived back at her apartment she found Will waiting for her with a bottle of champagne. It took only a glance at her tired, but happy face for him to know that things had gone well.

"The most intense and stressful hours I've ever spent," she told Will while sipping her drink. "I feel very strange. Tired and energetic at the same time, but definitely like celebrating."

"It's the 'fight-or-flight' thing," said Will. "You need some exercise."

After a walk by the river they went to an expensive restaurant and then to a night club where they drank more champagne and danced until closing time.

The following year passed very quickly for both Prudence and Will; he was submerged in his new novel and she in her research. Her selection of a dissertation topic turned out to have been a truly wise move; she was able to use her department's new electron microscope whenever it was free, almost any night or Saturday afternoon. Thus, unlike many graduate students, she was spared the frustration of having to build an apparatus. Likewise the availability of specimens from the Museum of Natural History eliminated the need for field work. In some circumstances such luck might have made other students jealous or irritated some of the older professors, but in no way did Prudence take unfair advantage of the situation. She worked long hours and, because of her natural dexterity, was soon a master of the fussy business of preparing samples for examination under an electron microscope. Despite her deep involvement in her project she could always find time to help less able students and was an avid participant in the department's weekly seminars.

After some nine months of studying photo micrographs she was able to show a correlation between certain types of crystal structures within the pores of microscopic, single-celled animals called foraminifera and the oil-bearing strata in which the specimens had been found. Although Dr. Cohen was himself no paleontologist he examined her work carefully and after consulting with friends at other institutions concluded that Prudence's work should be submitted to the international scientific journal *Micropaleontology*.

When word came back from the editors that her paper had been accepted for publication Dr. Cohen told her that her career as a scientist had begun and that she should begin writing up her dissertation. He also asked Will and Prudence to his home for dinner at which time he sprang a real surprise on them.

When a convenient moment arose Dr. Cohen took Will aside, handed him a glass of wine and told him about his plan for Prudence. "Given the acceptance of her paper, I think a successful defense of her dissertation is a foregone conclusion," he began. "So I expect her to be Dr. Billington before too long. So, I've recommended her for a post doctoral fellowship at the Centers for Disease Control down in Atlanta. It'd be different type of work than what she's been doing. It'd be a fairly prestigious appointment. Look good on her resume. Might open some doors for her. I'm not saying she'll get it. If she gets an offer, I hope you won't stand in the way."

"I'll be as supportive as I can," Will told him firmly. "Let's drink to Atlanta."

Two months later Prudence defended her dissertation, *Epitaxial Growth in the Pores of Foraminifera from Paleozoics Sediments*. After a short vacation she was on her way to Atlanta.

During her years as a graduate student Prudence had been careful not to flaunt her wealth, but once safely established as a fifty-something-year-old scientist she felt no great desire to live modestly. "I've paid my dues," she told Will unapologetically, and signed a one-year lease on a furnished, three—bedroom apartment. The plan was to use one bedroom as a study for Will and to keep another as a guestroom. The arrangement suited Will who decided that he should return to his earlier interest in the problems of migrant laborers. Thus he spent a good part of many weeks in Florida, but always returned to Atlanta for the weekend. When he talked on the telephone to Jane Wilson about what he was doing she promptly suggested that he write a proposal for a non-fiction book. Not only was the proposal accepted, but he also received a substantial advance from Taylor & Jones. Then came a big surprise. Taylor & Jones successfully completed the arrangements for a paperback edition of *Soldiers' Stories*. Soon, enough money rolled in to provide years of financial security given any kind of reasonable behavior.

Again, Jane Wilson proved to be an excellent, but blunt advisor. During a brief visit to New York they had lunch at her favorite Greek restaurant. She was explicit, "Will, I don't want you to be like so many writers and act like a drunken sailor. Just because you know all about artillery and horrible wounds and picking oranges doesn't mean you know shit about money. Don't blow your money. Get a real financial advisor. I want you to keep bringing me books to edit and not end up drunk and broke."

"Why are you bringing this up?" Will asked. "Have I given you any cause to worry?"

"Not yet, you haven't. I'm just trying to head off some problems before they arise. Hell, you've got a degree in literature. You must know about all the writers who drank too much, who had problems with dope. And money. Is a desperately poor writer more productive than a comfortable one? I doubt it."

"I don't know. What about Dostoyevsky? They he say he wrote some of his best stuff with creditors crowding around his door."

"I think that's a lot of bullshit. I'll tell you what this woman believes. Creative work, of any kind, in science, in the arts, in technology requires a certain amount of leisure, of security. There must be time for contemplation and, in the end, for polish. Just don't start boozing it up. And keep after the migrant labor thing."

Will promised to be a "good boy" and urged Jane to go easy on the *retsina*. Upon his return to Atlanta he followed her advice and did hire a financial consultant and, with one exception, continued to work hard on his new project. The exception was a two-week stint in Hollywood as a consultant on a movie about the Vietnam War. At first he was reluctant to accept the job, but did so in the end at the urging of Jane

Wilson. "Contacts in Hollywood won't hurt you," she told him over the telephone. "Maybe with a little luck we can sell somebody out there the movie rights to *Soldier's Stories.*"

Will did not much care for Hollywood or the project on which he had been asked to consult. He had serious qualms about producing something with "entertainment value" based on events that had caused him and so many thousands of others so much pain. He consoled himself with the thought that without his input the resulting movie would be even worse.

To his surprise he found Hollywood remarkably like the Army. The uniforms and titles were different, but the style was much the same. Instead of doing something to please the Colonel or the Captain things were done to please the Directors, the Stars and the Studio. Although pecking orders were not shown by insignia on collars and shoulders they were easily understood. Like the army there were sycophants and brass with big egos and instead of a *ides de camp* there were all kinds of quiet, but eager assistants. But most of all Will found himself resenting the handsome actors of his own age who had somehow escaped the war in comfort and safety while he and others were being shot at and wounded.

When he discussed these feelings with Prudence her comments were wise and generous. "Will, I have as much reason as anyone to be resentful, but I think it often took a lot of courage to resist the draft. And in the end, if you had had a younger brother, wouldn't you have urged him to avoid the draft? In the deepest part of me, I have to admit that I don't see the cowardice there so much as a reasonable response to an unreasonable demand."

Will did not reply. They sat quietly thinking about what Prudence had just said. Finally, she broke the silence, "Will, I've got a great job. I've got a wonderful man. I'm looking to the future. I want you to also."

Will nodded. "There'll always be scars, but I'm getting there. Don't forget I've promised Jane a good book on migrant labor."

Shortly after Will's return from California it was Prudence's turn for an invitation. She was sitting a her desk in the tiny office she shared with other "post-docs" when she received a phone call from the director of the geology department of a major oil company. "Dr. Billington," the man said, "You're a hard one to track down. I finally got your number from Dr. Cohen."

"I keep in touch with him, but why were you trying to find me?"

"Your paper in *Micropaleontology*. We'd like you to come out here and give a talk on what you found and, maybe, give us a few pointers. We're buying a new electron microscope. We can offer you an honorarium plus expenses."

Prudence was thrilled to find out that someone was actually interested in her paper and readily accepted the invitation. She also made it clear that it would be inappropriate for her to accept an honorarium, but that she could accept lodgings and transportation.

Like many women, even scientists, one of her first responses was, "What will I wear?" With Will's help she settled on an informal, but very expensive, khaki suit that would not have been inappropriate on a safari. With the thought that she might be given the chance to tour the company's refinery she selected some flat, boxy, comfortable brown walking shoes. She also received some unnecessary coaching from Will on her presentation.

"No need to be nervous. You've got great slides. Just put 'em up and explain what's on them." This had already been Prudence's plan and it worked well. Her only moments of nervousness came at the very start of her presentation when she looked around the conference room and saw that she was the only woman in a room full of tough looking men with sunburned and weather beaten faces. She immediately decided on a few straight forward, unpretentious opening remarks.

After acknowledging her introduction and expressing her gratitude for the invitation she told them, "I am primarily a biologist by training and make no pretense at great expertise in paleontology. I've always enjoyed looking at things under the microscope. When faced with the problem of selecting a topic for my dissertation I decided to play it safe, after all my name is Prudence. (By the way, I'm too fresh out of school to be called Dr Billington. Please call me Prudence or Pru.) I knew that that there was a large collection of foraminifera at the Museum of Natural History that was available to researchers and that our department had a new electron microscope. So I decided to take advantage of both. And, speaking frankly, I was much older than most all graduate students and just wanted to get through in the minimum of time. I discovered that there were a number of new shading techniques that had never been tried on forams before and, for that matter, that very little work had been done on them at really high magnifications. My first few slides will show you how the specimens were prepared and then we'll look at the results."

The talk turned out well. Between the carefully selected slides and Prudence's obvious, but unpretentious enthusiasm for the subject the audience was completely won over. It was followed by a lively discussion on possible ways of using her results to help find oil. When the meeting finally adjourned one of the company's microscopists escorted her to his laboratory where they had an enjoyable discussion on the fussy problems of specimen preparation. Next came lunch in the executive dinning room.

"Times are a changing," the Director told her. "Ten years ago we never saw a woman in a professional capacity in the oil business. Now we get a trickle of resumes all the time. From top graduates in chemical engineering. Want to work in the refinery or in one of the labs. Some of them, even out in the field on the rigs. Takes some getting used to. But for my money, or should I say, 'for the company's money,' brains are brains and if a woman is smarter than a man we want her, not him."

"I was lucky," Prudence commented, "I started out at an all-girl college and when I finally got to graduate school twenty-five years later I had an advisor with a psychiatrist wife and three smart daughters. I couldn't go wrong."

"I'm sure you could have stumbled along the way. It must have been tough going back to school after such a long break. I don't think I could do it."

"I doubt that. A large part of it is motivation. I was really motivated. I wanted to have my own lab, and I want to look at what I want to, when I want to. I'm happy to help people, but I don't want to be a helper. I hope that doesn't sound arrogant."

"No, it sounds like an entrepreneur talking. Sometimes I wish I'd left the company and started my own consulting business. Probably too late now, but maybe when I retire."

Because she had been married to an investment banker Prudence was used to meeting powerful men in their fifties or sixties and was not in the least bit intimidated by the Director. He was captivated.

"I'm going to turn you over to a guide for a tour of the refinery. After that I'd like to suggest that you come to our house for dinner. As it happens we're having a small party and I think you'd enjoy it. And I know my wife would enjoy meeting you."

"I'd love to accept," Prudence answered, "but I have plane reservations for this afternoon."

"Let me have my secretary fix that. Stay over and take the first plane out in the morning."

Prudence agreed and soon found herself in the hands of an assistant. It was easy to see why he had been selected as a tour guide. A bright, young chemical engineer, he was full of information about the refinery and was genuinely enthusiastic about his job. He also was thrilled to be escorting a beautiful woman and was sure that he was the envy of his colleagues. He fussed over her hard hat to make sure it fit comfortably and explained the advantages of the particular type of safety glasses they donned before entering the refinery. As for Prudence, it was a fascinating, new experience. She had had no real idea of the size or complexity of an oil refinery. They trudged through tunnels, climbed an endless number of steel stairways and even a few ladders. They visited two control rooms whose walls were festooned with a myriad of gages, switches, warning lights and diagrams. They sauntered along catwalks high above the ground. When she stopped to contemplate the open steel grill work of the stairs and catwalks she felt pleasantly vindicated in her choice of flat, comfortable shoes. She also enjoyed telling her young guide that from her courses in organic chemistry she had a pretty good idea of what happens in a distillation tower. When the tour finally ended he drove her back to her motel where she had a shower and a nap and changed for the party.

Because she had not expected to stay two nights in Oklahoma she had only brought one change of clothing. Not wanting to wear the khaki suit she had worn during her tour of the refinery, she was forced to wear the outfit she had traveled in from Atlanta, dark slacks and a long-sleeved blouse with wide, white, light-blue, and black stripes. She hoped it would not be too informal. She also worried about her shoes. They were her comfortable, everyday shoes with quarter-inch heels and little straps across the instep.

The "small party" turned out to be a combination barbecue and buffet. The Director cooked steaks out on a terrace by the swimming pool. His wife kept an eye on the buffet set up in the dinning room. Initially, the men with strong drinks in hand clustered around the Director while the women remained inside. Which group to join? Prudence wasn't sure. She would have liked to talk with some of the men, particularly some of the geologists, but felt a little shy about pushing her way into an all male group, especially here in a strange town. On the other hand, she felt a little shy about joining the women all of whom had probably known each other for years. The Director's wife solved her problem, first by steering her to the bar where she produced a strong, iced drink, and then by introducing her to some of the women.

They had, of course, already heard talk of a female microscopist from Atlanta and were eager to talk with her.

"How did you ever get into that field?" one young woman inquired. "What brought you out to Oklahoma?" and "Are you going to move here?" were typical questions. Prudence answered them all pleasantly, but found herself not very interested. She also had the uncomfortable feeling that she was 'being looked over.' But then, as the conversation drifted to other subjects, she learned that many of the women had lived in foreign lands such as Saudi Arabia or Indonesia, often under strange or uncomfortable circumstances. She warmed to them as they described the problems of raising and educating children and maintaining a home as they followed their husbands from assignment to assignment around the world. They also turned out to be much more interested in diseases and the microorganisms associated with them than with microscopic fossils and their potential role in the discovery of oil. They were just beginning to quiz Prudence about her work on *streptococcus* at the Centers for Disease Control when the Director approached and apologized.

"Ladies," he said, "I can't let you monopolize our guest. I've got a bunch of geologists who want to talk with her, but are too shy to come after her."

"Oh, no!" one of the women stated. "We were just getting to the good part. Promise to bring her back."

The director smiled. "I'll try to keep her around," he said and took Prudence's arm and guided her out onto the terrace. The conversation there turned around new techniques for finding oil. Prudence found it interesting and was thrilled to find herself accepted as a visiting scientist and fielded a number of questions about the origins of the samples she had used in her research.

When, all too soon, the party broke up she was able with real sincerity to tell the Director and his wife, "I had a wonderful time. Thank you so much for asking me."

They both shook her hand warmly and the Director said, "Thank you for coming. I hope we'll see you again."

Lying in her bed at the motel, too happy to sleep, she kept going over the day's events in her mind: the seminar, the tour of the refinery, and the party.

She wished that Will had been there to talk things over and to share in her happiness. Finally she decided that she must telephone him at his motel in Florida.

"I'm not surprised," he told her after she had related all the exhilarating experiences of the day.

"The party too. I enjoyed it. I enjoyed talking to the geologists, but I liked talking to some of the wives about their problems with children and traveling. I may be a scientist, but I'm still a woman."

"You didn't have to tell me that," Will replied. "I just wish I were there to take advantage of that fact."

"Me too," she answered. "I think we're going to have a great weekend."

She was right; their weekends in Atlanta were almost always good. One in particular would always standout in Will's memory. It was the occasion of Prudence's first major league baseball game. One evening as Will sat in a comfortable, old overstuffed chair reading the sports page the idea struck him.

"Pru, we should go to a baseball game sometime. What about next Saturday?"

Prudence put down the scientific journal she was reading and said "I've never even been to one."

"What, never been to a baseball game?"

"Not a big one."

"Okay," he almost shouted, "It's a date."

Prudence got up from the sofa where she had been reading and plunked herself down in Will's lap. "You sure have got me into a lot of firsts," she told him in a playful voice.

"Such as?"

"I seem to remember you dragging me into a great big tub of hot water and forcing me to be your mistress and then forcing me to go to school."

"Funny," he replied. "I don't remember it that way."

"How do you remember it?"

"I remember being squeezed into one corner of chipped old tub by a devastatingly attractive woman and then being forced to go to New York and be her sex slave."

"Will, do you really think I'm all that attractive?"

"I do."

"Would you still love me if I wasn't attractive?"

"That's a hard question."

"Oh?"

"If you weren't attractive, I wouldn't have been attracted and maybe never would have gotten to know you. But suppose you were plain, plain as a fence post, but somehow I'd found out how kind and competent and interesting you are, I'd have become just as hooked as I am now."

"That's sweet," she said and kissed him.

The following Saturday night they arrived early at the stadium and seated themselves comfortably along the first base line, just behind one of the dugouts. Will soon realized that Prudence had not been exaggerating when she had told him that she knew next to nothing about the game. When he tried to explain certain things to her he was never quite sure of what she really understood and what she was simply pretending to understand. He did notice that she never seemed bored and that she was paying close attention to everything. During the seventh inning they munched on hotdogs and guzzled down icy beer from enormous paper cups. In the last part of the ninth inning they stood with the rest of the crowd and cheered when the home team's star hit a ball over the fence.

Later, as they were climbing into bed Will said, "You've been pretty quiet. What did you really think of the game?"

"I was very glad that we went. I felt like the anthropologists we used to read about back in college. You know, the ones who investigated all the strange customs of primitive tribes."

"Primitive?"

"Not so much primitive as strange. Take all the spitting. I've never in my life seen so much spitting. And grown men no less. Evidently, somebody relaxed the taboo against spitting. And the costumes. What could be sillier on a hot night than the costumes. A lot of the players appeared to have well-developed bodies. Why not let them play in scanty clothing? In the Olympics athletes used to play in the nude. Why not something like that on a hot night? It sure would jazz up a slow moving game."

"They call them uniforms, not costumes," Will told her. "And they keep the players from getting scratched."

"Well, maybe. But if you changed the game around they could show off their bodies without getting scratched."

"This is fascinating," Will commented. "What else?"

"Now Will, I don't want to hurt your feelings."

"Go ahead."

"It reminds me of what one guy said about golf: Doing something foolish with equipment poorly designed for the purpose. It also reminded me a little bit of a bullfight with all the posturing and glowering. They even talked about bringing somebody out of a bull pen."

"But overall, did you like it?"

"I liked the spectacle of it. I liked being part of a crowd that was having a good time. That was nice. I liked being there with you. But I've got to say that no woman would ever have invented such a silly game."

"Women have their silly things too," Will came back quickly. "Take ballet. Is there anything sillier than a bunch of women parading around on tippy toes in their underwear?"

"The audience at least gets to see some good looking bodies that aren't all covered up in some silly uniform."

"Most of them are too undernourished for my taste. I'd rather hold you anytime."

"Really, Will?"

"Really," he answered as he turned off the light and reached for her.

Even more memorable than Prudence's introduction to night baseball was Will's introduction to boating. One Sunday morning, early in October, as they were sitting at the breakfast table finishing their coffees and reading the paper Prudence came upon an article about the beauty of autumn leaves in the Smoky Mountains.

"Will" she said, "lets go see the leaves. We can stop and visit Brenda McMahon on the way. I'm sure she would put us up, she has an enormous house. And I'll bet she can tell us the best places to see the leaves."

Will readily agreed and within a few moments Prudence was on the phone talking to the retired army nurse in Knoxville, Tennessee. After an exchange of pleasantries Prudence learned that her old friend was now the proud mother of six-month-old twin girls and could hardly wait to show them off. As for leaves, Brenda explained in no uncertain terms that the best way to look at autumn leaves in Tennessee is to avoid all the bumper-to-bumper car traffic in the mountains by taking a leisurely trip down the river in a houseboat.

"I've got my hands full with the babies, so I couldn't go with you. But I know you can handle a boat. Why don't you take ours?"

After a few routine "I couldn't do that." Prudence accepted the offer and asked, "What should we bring? What'll the weather be like?"

"Cool in the evening. Warm in the afternoon. And don't forget your bathing suits."

Two weeks later, on a perfect autumn afternoon, they arrived at Brenda's house on the Tennessee River. It had been over eight years since Will had seen her and he looked forward to seeing her again and wondered if she would remember him from among the many soldiers who had come through her wards.

When she appeared at the door to greet them she looked much as she had in Japan: copper hair, big freckles and voluptuous figure. She hugged them both. To Will she said, "I don't see many of my old patients. It's a treat to see you and in such good health! You were with us a long time, some tough times."

Will nodded as he thought of bedpans and being too weak to wipe his bottom. And of the catheters in his penis when his sphincter muscles froze up after surgery.

And of nausea from anesthetics and constipation from pain killers. And the unscratchable itching under hip-to-ankle casts.

"You're right," he answered. "There were some tough days, but you helped make them bearable. . . . Did you know that most of us were in love with you?"

"I guessed as much," she said. "After being around men, especially young men for twenty years you get to know what they're thinking about. Come and meet my husband and my girls."

She led them out onto a large terrace where Karl, her husband, was sipping a drink and enjoying the beginning of a long weekend. Their twin girls were asleep in a playpen. "We met just after I retired from the army and started working here in intensive care. Karl's a heart surgeon, a very good one. Nurses always know. Anyway, he liked the way I was taking care of his patients and thought I should take care of him. So here I am, retired again and then came the twins. I know I'm a bit old to have a baby. Some would say irresponsible. I don't know. They're healthy and so am I and I'm gong to be a good mother even if I'm going to look like a grandmother. I'm very happy."

Karl rose from his chair, stood beside his wife and put an arm around her shoulder. "You're fine, just fine," he said and kissed the top of her head. "Now let me get these folks a drink."

They spent the rest of the afternoon and a long evening talking and sipping a Tennessee whiskey with a smoky hint of the hickory barrels in which it had been aged. They ate a late dinner on the terrace where Karl cooked New York strips on a gas grill. A golden harvest moon arose from behind the trees on the opposite bank of the river, and from the patch of woods separating the house from the nearest neighbor came the haunting call of a whip-poor-will.

Among the topics they discussed was *Soldiers' Stories*. Brenda was quick to point out that she saw a certain resemblance between herself and one of the characters in the book. Will explained that the characters were supposed to be realistic and were partly composites and partly imaginary.

"If you do see a resemblance I hope you're not offended," he told her.

"No, the nurses come off pretty well. But I might as well say that I never had sex with a patient, ever."

"Suppose one of your colleagues had had an affair with a patient. What would you have thought of that?"

"Honestly, I'm not sure. If it didn't get in the way of her work I'd probably not worried about it."

"Speaking as a heart specialist," Karl commented, "I think I'd have been all for it. You'd be surprised how many patients ask me about sex. They're afraid that it will bring on another attack. In almost every case I tell them that it's going to be fine. And as far as I know it almost always is. I think lovemaking is very affirming and we all need affirming. Some more often than others, but we still need it, even surgeons."

"I'll drink to that," said Will and raised his glass.

The others followed suit. Karl rose and gave every one a refill and the conversation turned to other subjects as the golden moon grew smaller and turned to silver as it rose higher and higher in the clear autumn sky.

In the morning while Brenda was attending to the twins Karl briefed them on the operation of the houseboat and helped load provisions aboard.

"Not much can go wrong," he told them as he unrolled large scale charts of the river. "Generally, it's best to stay in the channels. Watch the buoys and stay away from any large towboats. They take a long distance to stop and make big waves. If you want to go into a cove to go swimming pull in slow and check the depth of the water with a pole as you go in. If you anchor, make sure it sets before you go to sleep. If you stop at a marina, make sure you creep in at a very low speed."

"I remember that from my sailing days," Prudence told him.

"Good, you won't have any trouble," he replied and shook hands with both of them. "See you in about four days."

Because all of Prudence's previous experience with boats had been with sea-going yachts she had been harboring a certain amount of disdain for freshwater boating. She had been too polite to express these feelings and soon forgot them altogether as she rapidly became accustomed to the convenience and spaciousness of the houseboat.

Its interior was divided into two spaces, a large comfortable room forward, which in addition to the controls of the boat, contained a two-burner gas stove, a stainless steel sink and an ice box. For dining there was a small oak table, and for reading and just lounging an overstuffed chair and a sofa. The sleeping quarters were aft and contained a small, but comfortable double bed, a closet and a dresser. A bathroom with a shower stall and a small, but efficient little toilet adjoined the sleeping area.

The front room opened onto a spacious covered deck where there were a number of folding canvas chairs and a charcoal grill. A ladder for swimmers could be hung over the side. Another ladder fixed to the side of the cabin allowed easy access to the roof.

As Brenda had advised them the boat was a perfect vehicle from which to look at autumn leaves: oaks, maples, poplars, hickories, and beeches all in bright yellow or gold slid by as they made their way down the river. Here and there, a slow poke provided a hint of green while others more advanced had descended into brown. Reds and pinks, not so numerous, provided a pleasing contrast and the tranquil, slow moving river reflected the deep blue of an impeccable October sky.

By early afternoon both travelers were famished and after carefully studying a chart maneuvered the boat into deep water alongside a deserted bank with overhanging trees. They tied a rope around an outstretched limb of an old oak and settled down for a leisurely lunch.

When they were almost finished Prudence said, "This seems like a good time to talk about something that's come up at the Center."

"Oh, what's that?"

"They want somebody to go to Paris for a year on an exchange program. I I'd like to be the one they send."

"That sounds exciting."

"But where would that leave us? I don't want to go alone. Would you come too?"

"Of course I'd come."

"But what about your advance on the migrant worker book?"

"It can wait. Jane will figure something out."

They sat in silence for a few moments thinking about different possibilities and ramifications. Finally Will got up and pulled his chair close to that of Prudence. He placed his hand over hers and said, "My turn to tell you what I've been thinking."

"Oh?"

"Pru, I think we should get married. We're happy together. I feel like we were made for each other."

To Will's surprise, Prudence's response was a weak smile and a stream of tears. "Will, that's so sweet. I'm touched that you would ask me, but I don't think it's a good idea. I do love you Will. I think you're a wonderful man: strong, kind, handsome. The problem is me. I'm too damn old. I feel like we're living on borrowed time."

"I don't care a thing about your age."

"But I do," Prudence replied.

"I may be younger, but I've got more gray hair and wrinkles," said Will proudly.

"That won't last."

Will sighed. "I feel a bit deflated."

"Well, I don't. It's not every day that an old widow gets such a great offer. Come on. You just need some *affirmation*." She rose from her chair and took Will's hand and gently pulled him inside and back to the aft cabin with its small, but comfortable double bed. Ever afterwards the word *affirmation* became their special code word for lovemaking.

When they finally emerged Will suggested that they wait until the following morning before proceeding farther down the river. Prudence agreed and suggested that they try out the fishing gear that Karl had insisted they take with them. Will having grown up as a city boy was a little reluctant and admitted that he had never caught a fish in his life.

"There's fishing and fishing," Prudence explained. "There's energetic fishing and lazy fishing."

"Oh? What's the difference?"

"In lazy fishing you bait a hook and attach the fishing line to a little float. When the float bobs up and down you jerk up on your pole and pull in the fish."

"I like the sound of lazy fishing. But what do you do if you catch one?"

"Ideally, you eat it."

The process was much as Prudence had described. They used corn kernels for bait and sat in comfortable deck chairs drinking wine and watching their little yellow floats for signs of a nibble. They were near the end of their second glass when Will's float began to bob up and down.

"Quick! Pull up," Prudence shouted.

Will did as he was told and soon was reeling in a sizeable fish which made his rod bend impressively. When the catch was finally on board it turned out to be a catfish, almost two feet long.

"Beginners luck," Prudence told Will in a tone of mock disgust.

Later when the fish had expired in a bucket of icy water Prudence gave an exhibition of her dexterity as she cleaned and filleted it for Will to cook on the charcoal grill. After dinner they sat silently watching the blue of the river turn into various shades of luminous bronze, and then, to a deep gray as early twilight changed to dusk and finally to dark. Under the clear autumn sky the surface of the river cooled quickly and the damp night air became chilly and penetrating. Instead of putting on sweaters they decided to retreat to the comfort of the irresistible double bed in the aft cabin.

When they awakened at first light and looked out the windows they were stunned to be barely able to see through the fog to the tree to which they were moored. The other bank was completely invisible. With all possibility of proceeding down the river temporarily out of the question they enjoyed a large and leisurely breakfast and then sank into the sofa and easy chair to read. Shortly before ten o'clock the sun burned away the fog to reveal another perfect autumn day and they resumed their journey.

After some hours of leaf watching Will suggested that they stop and go swimming. Looking at the chart they located a suitable cove about a half-mile farther down stream. When they were abreast of the cove they reduced speed and glided in. After dropping the anchor they donned their bathing suits and climbed down the swimming ladder into the clear, cool water. Prudence who had never before swam in freshwater other than in a pool was thrilled to find that the water did not sting her eyes. Will was relieved to find that the water was refreshing, but not cold enough to bother his leg. They both watched the boat closely to be sure that it was not drifting. When they had had enough they climbed back up the swimming ladder and picked up their towels.

"I'm going up on the roof and get some sun," Prudence announced, threw her towel onto the roof, and climbed up after it.

"I'll get some more stuff to lie on," Will said and entered the cabin. Once inside he spent a few minutes putting some beers into the ice chest and rummaging around to find some more towels. When he finally arrived on the roof of the cabin he was surprised to find that Prudence had taken advantage of a two-foot high, blue canvas screen and had removed her bathing suit.

"I haven't sunbathed in the nude since I was in college," she told him. "The sun is perfect, not too hot, not to weak. The air is just right."

"I've never sunbathed in the nude," said Will. "And I'm not about to start. I don't want to get my butt sunburned."

"Well, I hope you can stand seeing mine in broad daylight."

"I'm sure that at least one part of me can stand for it," Will answered quickly as he stretched out on top of a thick beach towel.

It took Prudence a few moments to reply, "Really Will, as a writer you should be able to say something wittier than that. I think you should be punished. But first, I'm going to check you for veracity." She rose up onto all fours and crawled the short distance to where Will was lying and straddled him. She leaned down and kissed him hard on the lips. Then she reached behind her and checked what was happening inside his bathing suit. "At least you weren't lying. Better take it off."

"What are you doing? We can't have an *affirmation* out here."

"Why not?"

"Somebody might see us."

"Who? We haven't seen a single person all day. And besides we've got the screen around us."

"I still feel a little bit shy."

"I don't. I feel like we're Adam and Eve before the fall."

"That's a funny remark for a biologist."

"Don't talk. Just take off your damn bathing suit. Everything will be fine."

He did as he was told and, as she had predicted, everything was fine. Later as they lay side-by-side on their towels Will began to laugh.

"Did you ever read the old Hemmingway story where the hero makes love to a partisan woman in a sleeping bag and she tells him that the earth moved?"

"Sure. We read that back at Vassar. We thought it was ridiculous."

"I used to think so," Will replied. "But I'm not so sure now. Didn't you feel the boat rocking under us? I'll always remember this as the day the boat rocked."

"So will I, sweetheart," she told him and hugged him tightly. "And now I'm going for another swim, this time in my birthday suit."

After a long swim they both felt chilled and donned sweatshirts and slacks. Will made coffee and they went out onto the deck and stood next to a rail while looking across the cove to a stand of trees whose autumn colors were perfectly reflected in the tranquil water. When Will turned toward Prudence he saw tears running down her cheeks.

"Pru, what's the matter?"

"I was thinking of an old poem. I think it was by Gerard Manley Hopkins. It was about a little girl watching the leaves fall."

"I know that one," Will exclaimed. "It starts with '*Margarét are you grieving over Goldengrove unleaving*' and ends with '*It is Margaret you mourn for.*' We studied Hopkins in graduate school. Pru, are the falling leaves making you sad?"

"Yes. I don't want anything to change. I don't want to get any older. I don't want to get gray hair and I don't want to get a dowager's hump."

"Wait a minute. I've got gray hair."

"That's different. You're a man. Yours looks *distingué*."

"Pru, I'd treasure you even if your hair were green. Or if you were bald."

"That's sweet. But I still don't want to get any older. Suppose I get too old to go to the lab."

"Sweetheart, very unlikely. I think you'll work for many years to come."

"I hope so. I love it. I like the variety, the challenge. The mysteries and the surprises. I like talking with other scientists. When I hear people grumbling about going to work, I feel sorry for them. I look forward to going to work every single day. I think I'm a very lucky person."

"We're both lucky, so let's enjoy the evening. Think about some of Hopkins' other poems. Do you know *Pied Beauty*? It's a celebration of textures and dappled things. Of the strange and wonderful things in God's creation. There's one line that reminds me of Brenda, it's in praise of '*Whatever is fickle, freckled (who knows how?)*' Don't ask me 'why', but I've always loved freckles. There's something primitive and sexy about them . . . . There are other lines in the poem that are more famous, one of them reminds me of you."

"Oh, what is it?"

"It's also a celebration, a celebration of the variety of tools. Of '*all trades, their tools and tackle and trim.*'"

"How does that apply to me?"

"I think of you in your lab with all your special tools and your microscopes and the pleasure you get from using them."

"So, you like celebrations?"

"That's right. I don't like laments and advice. I think a poem should be like a picture or an anecdote. And not too sing-songy. And it ought to have some beautiful or memorable lines."

"Give me an example of something memorable."

"Sure. My favorite is:

> *Oh fair enough are sky and plain,*
>   *But I know fairer far:*
> *Those are as beautiful again*
>   *That in the water are;*
>
> *The pools and rivers wash so clean*
>   *The trees and clouds and air,*
> *The like on earth was never seen,*
>   *And oh that I were there.*"

"That is beautiful," Prudence said as she moved next to him and put her arm around his waist. "But I think we have it better. Our trees don't need to be washed and our sky has no clouds."

On the following morning after the fog had lifted they headed back to Knoxville where they spent another night with Brenda and Karl before going on to Atlanta. Within several weeks of their return Prudence was offered the position in Paris. Due to health problems the current incumbent had cut short his assignment and Prudence was expected to arrive early in the coming January. Will was as thrilled as she was. The only person with reservations was Jane Wilson.

"Oh, shit," were her first words when Will informed her that he would be going with Prudence to Paris for a whole year. "What about your book? What about your advance?" she demanded.

"I don't think the problems of migrant laborers are going to go away any time soon," he told her. "Don't you think we can work out some kind of arrangement? Worst comes to worse, I could return the advance."

"That won't be necessary. My big worry is what are you going to be doing while Prudence is working. I'd hate to think of you sitting on your ass in some café drinking *pernod* and watching the *poules* strut by in their fancy suits and stiletto heels. You ought to have some kind of project. How about writing some articles on student unrest. I think I can help you get them placed."

"I don't think my French is good enough."

"Take some lessons."

As he had so often in the past Will followed Jane's advice and was soon enrolled in an intensive and expensive course of private lessons at a language school in down town Atlanta. His instructor was an earnest and punctilious little man with a toothbrush moustache and a crew cut. He invariably wore a white shirt with heavily starched collar and cuffs. Dark, almost-monochromatic neckties were always perfectly tied with a little dimple just under the knot. Will never learned if he could speak English. He started their first meeting with, "*Bonjour*" and then indicated with his hands that Will should respond. He did promptly with, "*Bonjour*."

The instructor then wrote his name, Jean Martin, on the blackboard and said, "*Je m'appelle Jean Martin*," and again indicated that Will should follow suit. He then spoke the only English words Will would ever hear him use in the many hours they would spend together: "Only French." This was followed by, "*Seulement Français*."

And so it went lesson after lesson. New words were introduced from an abundant supply of pictures. Where abstract concepts were required Monsieur Martin proved to be an excellent mime. He carefully structured the lessons to build on what Will remembered from his prep school days and to provide enough repetition of new words so that they would be remembered forever. By the end of December with the date of their departure to Paris approaching rapidly Will believed that he could handle the French involved in many everyday situations such as buying tickets, getting directions, making reservations, ordering food in a restaurant, visiting a doctor, or getting laundry done. To his great pleasure he found that he could easily read many of the simpler articles in the illustrated magazines that Monsieur Martin had given him to look for homework.

While Will was working hard on his French Prudence was wrapping up her work at the CDC and making travel arrangements. Because she had not, in several years, been to San Francisco to see her son Jack, or even seen one of her new grandchildren, she suggested to Will that they spend Christmas in San Francisco and proceed directly to Paris after the turn of the New Year. Jack, evidently with the approval of his wife, Claudia, suggested that they stay with them and the children for the holidays. Thus began a pleasant, but strange interlude.

Where women of Prudence's age were often confronted with the problem of assigning bedrooms to unmarried sons or daughters who appeared for the holidays with lovers Prudence herself presented a new problem: What do you do with a Granny who shows up with a young lover? What do you tell your children about Granny's activities? To Prudence's relief Claudia handled the situation as if it were in no way unusual. If the children had questions neither Will nor Prudence ever heard about them. The visit did, however, provide an opportunity for Will to see Prudence in a more maternal role than he had ever seen before.

She fussed over the two grandchildren and went to great pains to find appropriate Christmas presents for them. She helped Claudia with the cooking and the cleaning up. In the evenings, after the children were in bed, she cross-examined Jack about his job with one of San Francisco's major banks. For Will it was a happy, but at times a bittersweet occasion. Because of his father's premature death and his mother's health problems the Christmas holidays had often been very subdued in his home. And for the only time in his years with Prudence he had occasion to feel jealous.

For New Year's Eve Jack and Claudia had arranged a small, but gala party complete with a three-piece combo. For the occasion Prudence wore a perfectly-fitted, high-necked, dark-blue, Chinese-style dress with dramatic, thigh-high slits. Jack's boss, a high mucketymuck at the bank, was entranced and seemed to want to dance every dance with Prudence. For her part she seemed not only not to mind, but to welcome the attention.

Later, when they were in bed, Will said, "You certainly danced a lot with the banker."

"Will, are you jealous?" Prudence replied.

"Well, you certainly didn't seem to discourage him."

"He's a widower and obviously a bit lonely, especially at this time of the year. And he had a lot of interesting things to say, some of which will affect you."

"Such as?"

"There are new machines coming out called 'word processors'. He thinks they are going to replace the typewriter and he thinks that people who get in early are going to get very rich."

"Sound like science fiction."

"It does."

"Well, I'll give him one point. He looked like a terrific dancer."

"You're not so bad yourself," she answered and kissed him softly on the lips. "Happy New Year."

"Happy New Year, Pru," he replied and put his arms around her.

Two days later they were on a plane for Paris enjoying the complimentary champagne that came with their first class, Air France tickets. Several of the pretty flight attendants gave Will his first opportunity to try out his French. They were impressed. They were also curious about the attractive woman traveling with the handsome, younger man who evidently was her lover. In the hopes of finding out more about the couple they spent much more time than was necessary fussing over them and offering unneeded little services. Will enjoyed every minute of it. Prudence who was more than ready to snooze, was only slightly amused.

Once in Paris they took a cab directly to a small, but comfortable hotel on the Rue d'Anglais, conveniently located near the center of the city, just off of the Place Madeleine. The plan was to stay at the hotel until they had gotten over their jet lag and until they could take over the apartment recently vacated by Prudence's predecessor. It was a good plan. The staff at the hotel catered to their every need and was particularly friendly when they discovered that Will could carry on a simple conversation in French and that, for an American, his accent was unusually good. Will's favorite time at the hotel was breakfast where he discovered *croissantes, brioches*, and the perfect little loaves of bread called *petits pains*.

After two days of rest and acclimatization Prudence set out for the *Institute de Microbiologie* to meet her new colleagues and to learn about possible projects for the year; Will was to meet their new landlord, get a key to their apartment, and move in.

The person who turned over the key turned out to be the concierge, an elderly, bow-legged, stooped woman dressed completely in black. Due to some kind of dental problems her French was difficult to understand and Will had to ask her to repeat herself several times. His embarrassment was compounded as he followed her while she limped painfully up two flights of stairs to their apartment on the *deuxième étage*.

By American standards the apartment was primitive. It consisted of one large room and a tiny bathroom containing a toilet, a wash basin and a bidet.

Although Will had never seen a bidet before he had heard about them and knew enough not to ask a silly question about it. For a complete bath a tub was available down the hall and would be shared with other tenants. A small stove, a small refrigerator and a small kitchen table took up one corner of the apartment, and a handsome brass bedstead another. A thick eiderdown comforter lay neatly rolled at the foot of the bed. When he noticed it Will had not the slightest doubt that it would be needed: the room was finger-numbingly cold. When his elderly guide, evidently not immune to the cold, turned on the heat a loud and disagreeable clanking sound emerged from an undersized, cast iron radiator. The best part of the apartment was the view to the northwest with the cathedral of Notre Dame easily identifiable about a mile away. Will's almost-first thought about the apartment was, "What will Pru think of this place?"

By the time he had carried all of their suitcases up the two flights of stairs he no longer noticed the cold, and the clanking in the radiator had stopped. He put his electric typewriter on a worktable under the window with the view and plugged it into a newly purchased step-down transformer. He pulled up a chair and sat at the table looking out the window. He thought about Prudence and the apartment. It was certainly not like anything she had ever lived in. But the view was irresistible and the location, close to her institute and surrounded by restaurants and bookstores, was also a plus. After mulling things over for a while he decided to go out and get some groceries and flowers.

A sensual experience: the aroma of freshly baked bread, the texture of an unwrapped, golden loaf; the bright reds and yellows of artfully displayed apples and oranges; crisp-looking salad greens and the seductive scent of freshly ground coffee. And his French. He continued to be surprised and pleased by how well he could get along.

Upon his return to the apartment he arranged the flowers in an old pitcher and was just putting away the groceries when Prudence arrived.

"We go home for lunch!" she announced.

They embraced and Will gave her a quick tour. She laughed when she saw the bidet and said, "I don't think we can both get in at the same time."

As Will had expected she admired the view. She thanked him for the flowers and expressed her approval, "It's a bit Spartan, but the location is perfect. I think we will be very happy here."

"I agree," said Will. "Now let's go find a restaurant."

Over lunch Prudence described her new assignment. She was to assist in the identification of fungi associated with diseases of the skin and to work on the development of new staining techniques. Her boss, an attractive woman in her early forties was both a pathologist and a dermatologist. All the staff seemed friendly and helpful. Prudence's only worry was that she was expected to give a seminar on some of her previous work, in French.

Although Will's French was more than adequate for most day-to-day situations, he did not yet feel comfortable enough to conduct an interview in French and decided that more lessons were called for. The following day he enrolled in a language school where, as in Atlanta, he would have a one-and-a-half hour lesson every morning. He devoted afternoons to visiting museums and familiarizing himself with Paris. In the evening he and Prudence usually sampled one of the wide variety of restaurants which were within easy walking distance of their building. Because the landlord turned off the heat at an early hour the apartment was frequently cold and they enjoyed going to bed early and snuggling under the giant eiderdown. Most mornings Will prepared *café au lait* which he served to Prudence in bed along with her favorite *croissants*. Occasionally he prepared a lunch for her to take with her to the institute. And so the weeks passed quickly and happily. By early March Will believed that he was ready for some kind of project, but realized that he just wasn't really interested in doing an article on student unrest. At about the time that he had reached this conclusion he made a new friend who set him off onto a completely different tack.

One morning he arrived at the language school much too early for his lesson and was reading a French magazine in an anteroom when a tough looking man in his early forties entered and sat down. He too was early for a lesson, but as a teacher, not as a student. Speaking English with a heavy accent, which did not sound very French, the man asked Will if he was an American. And Will in turn asked the man if he was French.

"Yes and no," the man replied. "I am a French citizen, but I was born in Germany, just outside Berlin. I'm one of the German teachers here at the school. They like my accent. School policy: all teachers must be native speakers."

"A good policy," Will replied.

The man switched to an almost-accent-free French and said, "You must be studying French."

Will switched to French and replied, "Yes. I'm here in Paris for a year with my girl friend. She's working and I'm loafing."

The man switched back to English. "Your French is better than my English. Let me practice my English."

"Okay, but tell me how you happen to be a French citizen."

The man nodded. "After I escaped from East Germany I joined the Foreign Legion. Served ten years. They offer you citizenship when you get out."

"So that's where you learned French."

"And a lot of other things."

"Did you serve in Vietnam?"

"Yes, but we called it Indo China."

"How long?"

"Five years. And you? You look like the right age."

"I was there, almost a year and more than that in a hospital."

"You were wounded?"

"Yes, in the leg."

"A mine?"

"No, grenade."

"I was lucky. Never got hit. Got captured instead. At Dien Bien Phu."

"Dien Bien Phu? We studied that!"

"Studied it? Where?"

"At officer's training school. We learned that The French army was caught in a bowl surrounded by mountains. Over confident. Couldn't supply the place and the Communist artillery covered the landing zones."

"That's right. And then the generals decided to surrender before we all got killed. Communists took 6,000 prisoners, mostly legionnaires, and marched us off into the jungle. Treated us worse than dogs. Little water. Less food. No medical attention. If you got sick or straggled you died."

"We never learned what happened to the garrison."

"I'm sure you didn't. An ugly day for France, an ugly day for Europeans."

"What finally happened?"

"We were exchanged, those who survived. We got flown to Algeria in great big planes. No publicity. The government was ashamed of the whole thing."

"What a story. Then what?"

"I stayed in the legion another five years, until '59. Got my citizenship and went to live near Marseilles."

"And now Paris?"

"Met a woman on vacation. She talked me into coming up here. We got married. She's an accountant. Got this job through a friend of hers. They liked having someone who knows a lot of military slang. Then this job led to my being a waiter on Saturday nights at a restaurant that gets a large number of German businessmen and tourists."

At this point Will's teacher arrived and it was time for his lesson, but he was reluctant to discontinue the conversation and suggested that they might meet at another time.

"Certainly," replied the former legionnaire. "Come to the restaurant on Saturday night. Come at nine thirty. Bring your girl friend. Be hungry. It is German food: sauerbraten and schnitzels."

"I'll come," Will answered quickly, "but where is it?"

"It's in Mont Martre. It's called '*Le Petit Pomme de Terre*', the Little Potato." He handed Will a business card with the restaurant's name and a little sketch showing its location. "I am Gustaf Merkel," he announced and offered his hand to Will.

"And I am William Schmidt," said Will shaking the man's hand.

"A German name," the man remarked approvingly. "Till Saturday."

The evening at the Little Potato turned out to be a memorable occasion. One of the customs at the restaurant was for the waiters and other staff members to have a dinner together after the official closing time. Gustaf had arranged with the owner for Will and Prudence, as well as for his wife Nicole, to be included in the group. Unlike a regular meal at a restaurant there was no possibility of choosing from a menu. Instead each person was served a Wiener schnitzel with an assortment of vegetables. For drinks, a large carafe of red wine was placed in the center of the table. Nicole, petite, vivacious and very talkative reminded Will of a cheerleader. Like her husband she could get along well in English and her accent was charming.

The conversation sparkled and ranged from the light and frivolous to the most serious of topics. Nicole, an accountant, was interested in economic affairs and talked about the increasing economic integration of Europe that had begun with the coal and steel industries shortly after the end of the Second World War. And she talked about the increasing friendliness between France and Germany that would have seemed impossible just a few years earlier. "And look at me," she said while patting Gustaf on the arm. "Who would ever have thought I would marry a German?"

"And my parents, what would they have thought of a son becoming a French citizen?" Gustaf added.

From Europe the conversation drifted to the Far East and the war in Vietnam. The consensus at the table was that the United States should have learned from France's experience and not become involved. Arrogant and naïve were the words used to describe America's foreign policy. Will and Prudence listened carefully and found that they agreed with almost everything they had heard.

When the dinner was over and they had sipped a powerful brandy courtesy of the *patron* and it was obviously time to leave Will offered to pay but was turned down with, "When we come to America you pay."

Back in their cold apartment snuggling under the eiderdown Prudence announced, "We must ask them back."

"Here?" Will replied. "We've hardly got enough dishes for us much less for guests. And the table is too small. And what would we feed them? I'd bet Nicole is a great cook. Don't you feel intimidated to ask a Frenchwoman for dinner?"

"Not at all since you're going to be doing the cooking. As for dishes and utensils you can buy some. And the shopping will be a good experience."

"But what would we serve?"

"Something very American?"

"Like hamburgers and apple pie?"

"No, something fancier."

"I know. We used to have shrimp jambalaya in Florida. I think I can make that and rice."

"Sounds good, but what about dessert?"

"Easy. Baked bananas with brandy."

"I think you should practice on me before we invite them."

"Okay. But don't you think I should have some kind of confidence builder first?"

"Some sort of *affirmation*?"

"Just what I was thinking."

"Me too," she said and began to unbutton her pajama top.

The following Monday afternoon Will began his new project. His first task was to find a recipe. A bookstore specializing in English language books turned out to have an expensive and elaborately illustrated cookbook called "Creole Cooking."

The next problem was to translate the appropriate recipe. The words for *bay leaf*, *sassafras* and *okra* had never been part of Will's French lessons. His favorite old dictionary did not even have entries for *sassafras* and *okra*. When he consulted a newer dictionary he found that *sassafras* is the exact same word in both languages and, as he might have guessed, the word for *okra* is *gumbo*, similar to the name given by natives of Louisiana to a stew made from available ingredients and thickened with okra. Armed with his new words Will set out to find the special ingredients and the additional dishes and cooking utensils needed to make a Creole-style jambalaya.

The spices were easily located at an *épicerie* and the additional dishes and flatware at a department store, but one item remained difficult to find: a large iron pot. Although large casseroles with colorful ceramic coatings were easy to find and would almost certainly have served the purpose Will wanted to be a purist and use a plain iron pot, preferably one blackened by many years of use. In the end he found exactly what he wanted at the giant flea market located at the Porte de Clignancourt on the northern periphery of Paris. He lugged it home on the subway. The following day Will made his first jambalaya and proudly served it to Prudence. It was a success, but the rice, that usually accompanies the dish, was too gooey and called for some additional practice. Finally after several weeks Will felt that they were ready and asked the Merkels to come for a Sunday dinner.

To accompany the meal Will served a white Bordeaux which had been recommended to him by a waiter at a nearby restaurant. The party turned out to be a cook's dream. The guests were hungry, curious and appreciative. They were also surprised by the Spartan nature of the accommodations. And after a glass of wine became very talkative. With very little prodding Gustaf told of his experiences in escaping from East Germany and of his days in the legion. As he listened Will realized that he had stumbled onto material for several stories or perhaps even a book. When he mentioned the idea to Gustaf the former legionnaire was enthusiastic and offered to introduce Will to other veterans living in Paris. The end result was a short story that Jane Wilson with her ever-growing number of contacts in the publishing world helped place in a literary magazine. By mid summer he felt ready for another project.

One afternoon in late July as Will sat at a sidewalk café drinking a beer he bagan leafing through a lavishly illustrated magazine left behind by a previous customer. Because of his previous interest in New York's garment district an article on the latest women's fashions caught his eye. As he delved into the piece he began to wonder about the similarities and differences between the garment industries of Paris and New York. "Why shouldn't I do an article on it?" he asked himself. That night he talked the idea over with Prudence. She thought it sounded promising and suggested that he try to get some letters of introduction from some of his old contacts in the fashion industry. Will followed the suggestion and within several weeks found himself visiting the ateliers of some of the world's best known designers of women's clothing. Although he appreciated the friendly reception he received at almost every turn he found the experience disturbing. He hated most of the clothes. Almost invariably they seemed too extreme and too impractical. There were a few exceptions: severely conservative designs that reminded him of some of Prudence's evening wear. He found the models who exhibited the clothes equally unappealing: too thin, too pale and too earnest. At night he talked with Prudence about his observations.

"What kind of a woman would wear that stuff?" he asked her. "And the sickly looking models. Do they really help sell clothes?"

"I'm not sure. I don't think the really wild outfits are meant for sales. They're probably just meant to be attention getters, conversation pieces. I know I wouldn't be seen dead in some of them. As for the sickly looking models, I'm as confused as you are."

"Maybe they're really supposed to look sexless. Hell, I'd as soon put my arm around a baseball bat as some of the women I've seen in the last few days. It's hard to believe that you share a common gender."

From fashions the conversation drifted onto other subjects as Will began to air a growing curiosity about women in general. "What's it really like to be a woman? What's it like to have a baby?" he asked.

Prudence laughed. "Will, I thought you already knew the facts of life."

"I'm serious," he replied. "I know the facts. I want to know about the feelings."

And so she told him. She described the strange feelings of menarche and of menstruation. She told him about the inconveniences associated with pregnancy and the pains of childbirth and the satisfaction of breast-feeding. When she had finished with these topics she told Will about the tiresome condescension many bright women get from the unavoidable myriad of not-so-bright-men that seem to end up in positions of power or authority the world around. She also told him about the irritating lack of toilets in restrooms for women. When she had finally finished her lesson Will was silent for a long time.

Prudence was the first to speak. "Say something, Will. You're not asleep are you?"

Will rolled onto his side and propped himself up on one elbow. With his free hand he caressed her cheek. No, Sweetheart, I'm not asleep. Just thinking. Thinking about how much I've taken for granted. And about things that never occurred to me before."

"You're no worse than a lot of men and better than most, but that's not what I want to talk about"

"What do you want to talk about?"

"Well . . . . You've heard that 'turnabout is fair play'?"

"Yes."

"Well, I've been talking about some pretty personal things."

"True."

"Now it's my turn to hear about men."

"Okay."

"First, is it really true that men have pissing contests? To see who can piss the farthest?"

Will chuckled. "Pru, I can't tell if that's a serious question."

"Yes it's serious. I used to hear Peter and Jack joke about pissing contests and pissing into the wind. Now, tell me, do such things really happen?"

"To tell you the truth, I think it's more a figure of speech than anything else. Maybe such thing happen once in a while with younger boys, but I have no personal knowledge or first hand experience with pissing contests."

"Are you ready for another question?"

"Sure."

"Okay. What about masturbation? I've stumbled onto boys doing it. And I've read about it. It seems to be something of a taboo subject. Honestly, how prevalent is it?"

"*Prevalent?* I thought that was a word used by scientists when discussing diseases. I don't think that's a word I've ever used."

"Come on, Will. Fair is fair. Answer my question."

"Okay. The subject is shrouded in secrecy and hypocrisy. And the short answer is that it is very prevalent and that nobody likes to talk about it."

"And that includes you?"

"And that includes me."

"Interesting," she said as she put an arm across his chest and her head on his shoulder and was soon sound asleep. Will lay quietly beside her thinking about all the things they had talked about and did not go to sleep for a long time.

Will's education continued when he stumbled onto a biography of Marie Curie in a secondhand bookstore. Like most non-scientists, Will had only a vague idea about Pierre and Marie Curie, but his curiosity about them had been piqued because he frequently walked down Rue Pierre et Marie Curie on his way to the Métro. The more he read about them the more interested he became, but it was not the facts of their scientific discoveries which he found so fascinating, but the details of their personal lives. He was particularly fascinated by the photographs.

One of the strangest pictures in his book was of a buxom, young Marie Sklodowska who with the hint of a double chin looked completely unlike the lean, focused scientist the world would come to know. He was surprised to learn that before leaving Poland to study in France she had worked as a governess and had fallen in love with her employer's son and had been hurt by his family's rejection. Will wondered about the level of intimacy that had existed between them. Had she been a virgin when she left Poland? Will suspected that she had. His evidence for this suspicion was non-existent and depended on the biographer's assertion that something wonderful had happened to Pierre and Marie Curie on their wedding trip. He studied the famous photograph of the honeymooners with their bicycles.

Deeper into the book he learned the little-known fact that Pierre's father, following the death of his wife, had moved in with the couple and had been a major provider of child care thus making it easier for his talented daughter-in-law to pursue her investigations in chemistry and physics. When he discussed this unusual arrangement with Prudence her comment was, "Without some kind of childcare, some kind of backup she never would have discovered radium. Somebody else would have."

Although Will would be influenced by this conversation for the rest of his life he did not immediately say anything.

"Have you come to the part about her affair yet?" Prudence asked him.

"Affair?"

"Some years after Pierre's death. People were scandalized. Men could do anything. But not women. What hypocrisy! Why shouldn't a vigorous middle-aged widow want to have a man in her bed? I know I did."

"Well, I'm glad you pulled me and not some other guy into your bed."

"I don't remember pulling you into my bed. I was seduced by a woman-hungry man and dragged into a big old bathtub."

Will smiled and put his arms around her. "Speaking of tubs," he said, "I'm really getting tired of the bidet and of having to go down the hall for a bath."

"When we get back to New York you can spend all day in the bath. I heard from Dr. Cohen. He wants me to come and work in his group. A research staff position. No teaching. Not a tenure track position."

"Do you want it?"

"Definitely. I don't need tenure. I've got plenty of money. If they don't treat me well I can set up my own lab. But what about you? Do you want to go back to New York?"

"I'll be ready when you are."

"My year'll be up in December. Let's spend Christmas in New York."

"Agreed."

In the following weeks Prudence wrapped up her work at the *Institute de Microbiologie* and collaborated with her director in the preparation of a scientific paper on the microscopic examination of fungi removed from the lungs of men who had died of a particularly vicious form of pneumonia. Will made the travel arrangements. They landed in New York on Christmas Eve.

By the middle of January they were both hard at work, Will on his unfinished book and Prudence on a new project with Dr. Cohen. It appeared to be a happy time. They visited old friends and went to the theater and to concerts. Despite their gastronomic adventures in Paris they even enjoyed going to their favorite old restaurants. But things were not quite right for Prudence. Although she found her new research project interesting and challenging, she was bothered by a feeling of malaise. When she looked in the mirror she saw signs of wrinkles she had never noticed before. Two little puffy places appeared near the corners of her lips. Her hair which had been glossy black suddenly was streaked with gray. Worst of all was the message from the bathroom scale; her weight which had never varied by more than a pound or two from 147 pounds had suddenly risen to 153. When she complained about these matters to Will, he was unimpressed.

"Lots of women are putting colored streaks in their hair. A few gray hairs will only make you more fashionable."

"And my weight. I'm getting fat."

"Pru, that's absolute baloney. Even if you gained a lot more weight you'd still be one of the best looking women in New York." Definitely, the wrong thing to say.

"I knew it," Prudence replied in a peevish voice. "*More weight!* So you think I'm getting fat."

"That's not what I said."

"I know what you said."

"Hey, wait a minute, that's the angriest thing you've ever said to me."

By this time the tears were rolling down. "I'm sorry, Will. I'm just not feeling myself. Forgive me?"

"Don't see much to forgive," he said and enveloped her in his arms.

As the weeks and months rolled by Prudence's disposition improved, but she was not as energetic as she used to be. Although she was always ready for bed by bedtime, she no longer initiated any sexual activity. If Will wanted to make love, she always responded enthusiastically and continued to take pleasure in pleasing him. Will noticed nothing. He continued to enjoy every aspect of their lovemaking and had no idea that their time together was drawing to an end.

One evening, after they had been back in New York for almost a year, Prudence told Will that it was time for them both to go their separate ways.

"What are you talking about?" Will demanded.

"Will our relationship is holding you back. Stunting your growth?"

"Stunting my growth?"

"You should have a wife, a real wife, not a mistress."

"I've asked you before. Why can't we get married?"

"I am too damned old for you Will."

"Can't I decide that for myself?"

"No."

"Why not?"

"You just can't be objective."

"Maybe I don't care about *objective*."

"Well I do. Think about it Will! You don't want to have to be shepherding an old wife around when you're just approaching middle age."

"I think any man would be lucky to be shepherding you around."

"That's sweet, Will. But what about when I get a widow's hump? Or start drooling or leaking? Or get dried up as a prune?"

"I'm not worried."

"You should be."

"Didn't you ever hear, '*Love's not love that alters when it alteration finds*'?"

"I remember reading it in an English course back at Vassar. It's from one of Shakespeare's sonnets. And I can tell you that it was written when life expectancy was in the thirties. And Shakespeare didn't do so well by his own wife."

"That's irrelevant."

"I don't think so. Wasn't his wife older than he was?"

"I think so. But I still think it's irrelevant," Will insisted."

"I don't want to be around when you find a younger woman."

"Pru, I can't imagine any woman who could compete with you."

"Well, I can and I don't want to be around. And I don't want you taking care of me?"

"Taking care of you? What are you talking about?"

"Don't be dense Will. You are a vigorous man just entering middle age. You don't need to be looking out for an old woman."

"I'm not afraid of responsibility."

"It'd be the wrong kind of responsibility. You need a wife and children."

"I don't know what to say. This comes as a Hell of a surprise."

"Don't say anything. Just listen. When we first got together you were my guide. You advised me about graduate school. You'd been there and I hadn't. I listened to you. Now it's my turn to be the advisor. I love you, but there are a lot of things I can't do for you. I can't give you a child. And soon I won't be able to keep up with you. I'll want to go to bed when you want to go out or I'll want to read when you want to go hiking. Trust me, I know what I'm talking about. I was married to an older man."

"I still don't know what to say."

"This may sound awful, Will, but I know what I'm talking about. And I truly believe I know what's best for you."

"Best for me! . . . That sounds pompous."

"Will, I *am* a generation older than you."

"Since our time in Connecticut I've never felt that way. I felt protective of you. You seemed innocent and vulnerable."

"I know you did. And I appreciated your encouragement. But this is a different time."

"So what do you want to do?"

"I want us to go our separate ways. I'm going out to the coast to see Jack and Claudia. If you want to keep the apartment you can. If you don't, I want you to find another place while I'm gone."

"I sure don't want to live here by myself."

"I don't either. We'll get rid of it."

"Pru, are you sure you know what you're doing?"

"Yes, I've thought a lot about it. I think it's for the best, especially in the long run."

"Answer me this. Are you getting tired of me Pru.?"

"No, not at all."

"After this conversation, don't you think I deserve some special *affirmation*?"

Prudence smiled. "You're still my favorite sex fiend."

"Good," said Will and took her hand and led her toward the bedroom.

An hour later as they lay naked side by side covered only by a sheet Will said, "I don't care what you think about age. You sure have a beautiful body."

"I'm gaining weight and I don't like it."

Will sat up and yanked the sheet away and studied her body. "Pru, there's not a blemish on you," he told her as he ran his hand lightly over the small fold of fat just below her navel. "And I think your tiny bit of tummy is delectable." He wiggled down in the bed, turned onto hands and knees, leaned down, and kissed her belly. Next came a few gentle nibbles.

At this point Prudence reached down and put both hands on his jaw bone, just under his ears and pulled him forward on top of her. After a long kiss Will rolled to one side and pulled Prudence on top of him. He ran his hands down her back until they were squarely on top of her buttocks. "Can I tell you something?" he whispered into her ear.

"Sure," she whispered back. "If it's important?"

"Very. I hate not having a nice sounding English word for this part of a woman's anatomy. I think the French do so much better with *derrière*."

"You'll always be my special wordsmith." she replied and kissed him. And so they made love for the last time.

The following afternoon Will rode with Prudence to the airport and put her on a plane to San Francisco. Initially, he had hoped that she would change her mind, but as the days went by he became more and more convinced that that was not ever going to happen and began making plans for a different life. In the end he decided to return to Gainesville and finish writing his latest book in Florida. During the spring semester the chairman of the English department at the university offered him a job as adjunct faculty member. Will accepted readily and found that teaching and writing made a nice mix. Although he enjoyed talking about books and ideas with graduate students and other faculty members, he did not meet any women that were of more than passing interest. There seemed to be something wrong with all of them. Some talked too much and said too little. Some didn't talk enough. He found himself irritated by the frivolity of some and the seriousness of others. In one case, he just couldn't stand one woman's scent.

And so two professionally productive years passed without any personal involvement. At he beginning of his third year in Florida he had occasion to visit New York to talk to Jane Wilson about a new project. After a luncheon at her still-favorite Greek restaurant she invited him to a party to be given by Taylor & Jones the following evening.

Among the guests at the party was a young lawyer involved in defending Taylor & Jones against a libel suit. Will noticed her standing by herself next to the punch bowl and was immediately attracted and introduced himself. Her name was Emily Richardson. If she knew who Will was or had ever read one of his books she certainly didn't let on. This only served to make her more attractive; Will felt no need for mindless adulation. Not only did he like the shape of her face, he immediately felt comfortable with her conservative dark dress which contrasted well with her jaw-length blonde hair. And her scent was subtle and intriguing. But best of all she turned out to be interesting and to be doing interesting work. At twenty-eight she was 3 years out of law school and was enthusiastic about working on first amendment and related issues in the publishing world.

On their first date, which took place the following evening, they spent a lot of time talking about copyrights. Will enjoyed listening, something many of the young men she saw in the course of her work were not good at.

She had what Will thought to be the perfect middle-American voice. From her accent he had guessed that she had grown up in Ohio and was quietly pleased with himself when he found out that he was right.

Back in Florida, Will continued to think about Emily and began to make long distance calls to her once or twice a week. He sensed that his calls were always welcomed and wished that they could talk face-to-face. After a month had gone by he became increasingly impatient with this arrangement and found an excuse for another visit to New York. Things went well and he was soon traveling to New York several times a month. Finally, over the Thanksgiving weekend, he asked her to marry him.

Her answer was an enthusiastic, "Yes, but on one condition."

"Oh, what?"

"That you not ask me to give up my job and move to Florida."

Will laughed.

"What are you laughing about?"

"Only in relief. You scared me for a moment."

"Scared you?"

"Yes, I thought you were going to ask me to perform some kind of Herculean task."

"You don't have any problem then, with me keeping my job in New York?"

"No, Sweetheart. On the contrary. I'd be sorry if you wanted to give it up. I'm proud of what you do and happy that we're somewhat involved in the same world."

The wedding took place in Cincinnati, Ohio between Christmas and New Years. Will resigned from his job in Florida and happily moved back to New York. He found his young wife as intriguing in bed as she was in describing an interesting law case. Unlike Prudence she was shy and modest. And unlike Prudence, who had been muscular and cool to the touch, Emily was voluptuous and hot to the touch. She reminded Will of a nude by Renoir. He kept all such thoughts and comparisons to himself. In fact, being busy with their careers and growing family, and being happy with each other, they had for twenty years never talked about previous romances or affairs until the day after Will's sixtieth birthday party.

One afternoon, two weeks after the memorial service for Prudence, a package arrived from Jack Billington. It contained a letter explaining that as executor to her estate he had had to clean out her desk and had found the enclosed glass sculpture along with a bundle of notes and cards. From the content of the notes it was obvious that the sculpture had been a present from Will. According to Jack, it had been one of Prudence's most treasured possessions. Also included in the package was a letter addressed to Will in a handwriting he had not seen in many years, but which he recognized immediately.

He removed the glass object from the box, carefully removed its elaborate wrapping, and set it down on its simple wooden stand. There in front of him was a foot-long glass model of a paramecium complete with vacuoles, a gullet opening, and cilia. The vacuoles were ruby colored bubbles that the artist had somehow encapsulated in the main body of the model. The cilia were gold wires and had evidently been inserted into the glass while it had been in a near molten condition. Although it had been many years since he had seen the model, he remembered clearly the day in Paris that he had bought it as a birthday present for Prudence. It had made a great hit:

"It's beautiful and so imaginative. How many men would have thought to give a woman a paramecium? I love it."

Prudence had also liked the card that had accompanied the gift and had kept it. It was on top of the bundle that had accompanied the package. Will opened it and read what he had written twenty-five years ago:

Sweetheart,

When I saw this model it reminded me immediately of you, not just because you're a biologist, but because you're so beautiful and efficient and deliciously primitive all at the same time. Happy Birth Day!

Love, Will.

61

Next Will opened the letter from Prudence:

Dearest Will:

Time is running out for me and I wanted to communicate with you at least one more time. Although we have not seen each other for many years I have from time to time heard news of you. I understand that you married a kind, bright and beautiful woman with whom you have two fine daughters. I think this proves that I made the right decision to break off our affair all those years ago. (I still hate the word 'relationship'.) And I want you to know that the years we were together were among the happiest of my life and that I doubt that I would have ever gone to graduate school without your encouragement. You were a wonderfully sexy lover and a great traveling companion. I have never forgotten the time we went 'skinny dipping' in that beautiful cove on the Tennessee River or the times we snuggled under the giant eiderdown in our cold little room in Paris. If you ever think of those days I hope you do with some of the same pleasure they give me. And I hope that when and if you ever think of me you will not feel that I wasted too much of your time and that you will be glad that we parted when we did.

With love,
Prudence

After reading and rereading Prudence's letter Will sat quietly at his desk and pondered its contents. He was glad that Prudence had been happy during their time together. He too had been happy. But he could not say that their days together had been his happiest times. Prudence had been right: he had needed a wife and a family. He had needed more responsibility than that offered by a rich, beautiful older woman. "But what about her?" Had she needed the companionship of an older man? Had she needed the special companionship offered by someone working in the same field? Or had she ended the affair because she had put his interests and needs ahead of her own? His reverie was interrupted by the telephone. It was Emily.

"Will," she said, "You sound far away. Is anything wrong?"

"No, Sweetheart, I was just daydreaming."

"Okay, but don't forget that we're going out tonight."

"I'll be ready when you get back."

"Good. Love you."

"Love you too."

"Bye."

"Bye."

Will put the model of the paramecium down on one corner of Prudence's letter as a paper weight and went to get ready to go out. Because he had plenty of time he decided to have a leisurely bath. Once in the tub his mind wandered back to the day that he and Prudence had bathed together during the still-remembered Valentine's Day blizzard. Relaxed by the hot water and feeling unhurried he dozed off and awakened only when the water had become cold, almost a half-hour later. He hurried into the bedroom and had just finished dressing when Emily came in, earlier than expected.

"Hello, Sweetheart," he greeted her.

"Don't Sweetheart me," she replied in angry voice.

"What's the matter?"

"I stopped in your study to put some papers on your desk and I saw that thing."

"The paramecium?"

"Whatever it was. And I saw some papers under it and I thought they might explain what it was. But one of them was a letter to you. I read it. I know I shouldn't have. But it was already in my hands."

"I don't mind," Will replied, "I'd have shown it to you if you'd asked. I haven't done anything I'm ashamed of."

"I think you have."

"What have I done?"

"Your affair with that woman, that biologist."

"That was long ago, long before I met you."

"And how long did it last? Six days? Six weeks? Six months? Six years?"

"Well it wasn't quite six years."

"Will, that's horrible. That's a big part of your life. That's like having been married and not telling your wife that you had been married before."

"I don't see it that way. I had no legal obligation to Prudence and she had none to me. And there were obviously no children involved. No money involved."

"You lived with a woman for six years and felt no responsibility? Did you ditch her for a younger woman?"

"Emily, that's beneath you and you know it's not true. You read her letter. It was her idea to end things. Not mine. I loved her very much and was willing to accept whatever problems came with her getting older. More than once I asked her to marry me."

"You asked her to marry you?"

"Yes, and she turned me down because she thought she was too old."

"So now I find out that I was your second choice."

"Emily, that's ridiculous. It wasn't a matter of choice. I met you years after Prudence had broken off our affair."

"I still don't like it. And the part about Paris and 'skinny dipping.' I'm jealous."

"You have nothing to be jealous over. And what about you? Surely you must have had some happy experiences before we met. I thought you were irresistible the first time I met you. Other men must have been attracted to you."

"I suppose some were, but none of them ever took me "skinny dipping" or to Paris. And neither have you."

"I'd be happy to go anywhere with you anytime, but you're always working."

"I'd at least like to be asked. And this Prudence. Was she better looking than me? Was she better in bed?"

"Emily, that's not the kind of question a person should ask?"

"Why the Hell not?"

"It's too personal."

"Too personal ? You're my husband. I feel like I have the right to ask you anything I want."

"Maybe, but you're a lawyer. You know the rules of cross-examination. You shouldn't ask a question if you don't know the answer."

"This isn't a courtroom. Tell me. Was she more attractive?"

"It's hard to say. Different styles. Different colors. She had dark hair; you have blonde."

"Tell me!"

"Haven't you heard? Gentlemen prefer blondes."

"Don't be evasive Will."

"In all honesty, it's close, but you come out ahead."

"Good. But did you love her more than me?"

"That's a silly question."

"Why silly? I want to know."

"What do you think? You're the mother of my children. We've been together, harmoniously for twenty years. Have I ever given you cause to doubt my loyalty? Haven't I always been there for you when you needed me? Why do you have to ask?"

"I just do. I'm a lawyer. Remember? I'm supposed to be competitive."

"Okay then. I think you are the best. And I love you more than anyone else, anywhere, any time."

"Good," she said and put her arms around him and hugged him. "I think I knew it all along, just needed to hear you say so."

Will said nothing and returned her hug.

After a few moments she whispered, "I love you Will, but I need to get ready for the party." Will left her to change and went to his study where he carefully wrapped up the paramecium and put it and the bundle of notes and cards that had come with it into the back of the bottom drawer of his desk. And though Will continued to think about Prudence once in a while, he and Emily never discussed her or the affair or the paramecium ever again.

CPSIA information can be obtained at www.ICGtesting.com
Printed in the USA
LVOW121650271012

304726LV00002B/1/P